A Magical Highland Solstice

by

Mary Morgan

A Magical Highland Solstice

Cover Art by *Debbie Taylor*

The Wild Rose Press, Inc.
PO Box 708
Adams Basin, NY 14410-0708
Visit us at www.thewildrosepress.com

Publishing History
First Fantasy Rose Edition, 2016
Print ISBN 978-1-5092-1125-8
Digital ISBN 978-1-5092-1126-5

Published in the United States of America

With each steady trot, her body swayed
and Cormac tried to focus on the *road. The castle. Fighting in the lists. Bathing in the icy waters of the loch.* Anything but the soft curves of the lass's body pressing against his own. What was wrong with him? He prided himself on being a man always in control of his emotions—especially his lustful ones. Yet, now he found himself confused, tongue-tied, and his gut twisted into knots.

So deep in his thoughts, he did not notice Fingal veering off the main road until the lass let out a giggle. She had the most musical sound, and he found himself smiling. Guiding his horse back to the path, he could hear his men doing their best to contain themselves. A glance back confirmed William was coughing loudly and Gordon trying his best not to fall off his horse.

"I swear Fingal, I am tempted to trade ye in for another horse. Ye must be going blind, or worse, old."

His horse let out a large snort.

Eve clicked her tongue in disapproval. "For shame, Mr. Murray. How cruel. I think he's a kind animal. Perhaps it's the man holding the reins who can't see clearly the path in front of him?"

The lass was quick with the wit, he mused. "I dinnae ken your word, but ye may call me Cormac." He leaned near her again. "And I can assure ye, I am nae blind, nor old."

Dedication

For my siblings
Mimi, Vici, and Randy with love.
My fondest memories of the holidays
were spent with you.

Prologue

Once every hundred years, two souls are brought together through the veil of time. They are deemed the chosen ones by the Fae. Through their acts of kindness, generosity, and love to others, they often neglect to find their one true love. Their devotion to aiding others blinds them to their own happiness, leaving them alone.

It is during the season of the Winter Solstice—a time of great magic and love that the Fae search for these worthy to receive their gift. Faery guardians will clear the path and open the doors between the realms, so the two lovers can meet. Their souls destined to become one with each other.

Yet, time is fleeting and only the strongest and purest of heart will be able to capture the spark of love. If the ember ceases to grow, then on the stroke of midnight on the Winter Solstice the two lovers will be returned to their own time. The doors of past and present to be closed forever.

In this year, 2016, the Fae have chosen Cormac Blaine Murray and Eve Catherine Brannigan to receive this special blessing—a chance of love—*everlasting*.

When the light of true love whispers in their hearts, Cormac and Eve must trust and believe in the magic that brought them together before the sands of time vanish into the mists of the Highlands.

Chapter One

Castle Creag—December 1207

"Bind together the pine, cedar, oak, and birch to create the incense of the season."

If he could, Cormac would flee to the hills to rid himself of the latest disaster in the kitchens. His cook, Moira, usually a calm and even-tempered woman, had become the target of the latest in a series of mischief between two of the castle's lads. Both of whom now stood before him—shouting and accusing the other of plotting to let a few of the sheep roam into the kitchens. All done in an effort to fetch a couple of freshly baked tarts. Their folly had caused Moira to trip over one of the ewes and injure her leg, and burn her arms.

Was it too much to ask for a few moments of peace and solitude while he ate his meal? Perchance, if he closed his eyes, the lads would ignore him and take their argument out into the bailey. A wishful thought he swiftly pushed aside.

"Ye are full of horse dung! I never told ye to bring the sheep. I said the dogs!" yelled Bran.

"Are ye daft? I told ye I would nae bring in the laird's dog or any other of the hounds," protested Ranald.

Bran snarled at him. "Ye were scared of what the

laird would do to ye."

Cormac pinched the bridge of his nose to ward off the impending pain creeping in behind his eyes. "Enough!" he roared. "I can tell by your arguing in front of me—*your laird*—that neither of ye has any remorse from this mishap."

Both lads immediately went quiet and bowed their heads.

"'Tis shameful!"

Both nodded silently in agreement.

"Ye should not be allowed to step foot inside the castle. Mayhap I shall banish ye to the stables for the rest of the month."

"And miss the Yule feasting?" both protested in unison.

Cormac crossed his arms over his chest, glaring at them. In his heart, he would never banish anyone to the cold, foremost a child, but he would not let the lads ken this yet. "Pray tell, what would ye have me do? Surely, ye dinnae believe ye can be forgiven so easily?"

Ranald narrowed his eyes in thought, and Bran started to tap his foot, which told Cormac they were fully prepared to come to some sort of deal.

Bran raised his hand. "If I may be allowed to speak, my laird?"

"Granted," stated Cormac.

The lad stole a glance at Ranald. "First, we will clean both kitchens. From hearth and stone." He paused and scratched at his chin.

"Continue."

"Then we will see to the kitchen duties and tend to Moira."

Ranald gave Bran a scathing look.

"Do ye deem it wise to be in the verra place that would tempt ye to snatch food?" Cormac held up his hand when the lad started to utter a protest. "I agree to the first part of your terms. But for the second, ye will clean all muck from every place inside and outside the castle. From the stables, to the urinal pots. Since ye have mentioned Yule, this is a time of preparation and we need all hands to help." Watching as their faces grimaced and then went to wretched horror, he fought the smile forming on his own face. "Are we in agreement?"

"Aye," muttered Bran.

"Are ye saying we have to do this for one day, or for the entire month?" asked Ranald.

The truth revealed itself with the lad's question. Cormac knew him to be the leader in this devious plan. "For as long as I deem necessary. What say ye?"

Ranald's shoulders slumped. "Aye."

"Good! Now go and begin cleaning the kitchens. When ye are done, seek me out. If not done to how I ken Moira likes the place, ye will start over. Understood?"

"Aye," both mumbled in unison.

"Off with ye."

Cormac watched their slow retreat from the Great Hall. Placing both his hands on the table, he whispered, "What am I going to do now?" With no cook, he would have to rely on one of the young lasses.

One of his men, Gordon, stepped inside. "Have they been properly punished?"

Waving the man over, Cormac poured some wine into a mug and handed it to him. "Aye, but not as severely as ye may think."

Taking the mug, Gordon sat down. "What? Ye are not going to tie them to a post in front of the gates for all to witness their punishment for their heinous crime?"

"Worse. Not merely are they cleaning the kitchens to my approval, but every other place full of muck—from stables to urinal pots."

Gordon choked on his wine. Wiping his mouth with the back of his hand, he shook his head. "Aye, 'tis far worse. No one will want to be near the lads' stench. For how long will they be punished?"

Rubbing his hand over his chin, Cormac shrugged. "Cannae say." Sitting down, he poured some wine into his mug. "Did ye see the place?"

"I ken all have taken a peek inside the kitchens."

Cormac pointed a finger at the man. "Next, the bards will be filling the hall with the tale of two lads."

"Och, a story for the ages." Gordon laughed. "What are ye going to do? We have nae cook and 'tis almost Yule."

"Do not remind me," he groaned and took a large swallow of wine.

"Ye could always send for someone in one of the villages."

"Ye ken well there is no one."

Gordon leaned his arms on the table. "What about one of the lasses that helped Moira? Surely they can be of some service."

"Have ye not seen them? They are inexperienced cooks—young and foolish. Burning most of the meals. Neither is ready to feed an army of men, women, and children." Cormac rubbed his eyes feeling the headache go from a dull ache to throbbing pain.

Sitting back in his chair, Gordon finished his wine. "Let me search the villages. Perchance there is someone there who can help."

He gave the man an incredulous look. "And have them leave their family during the Yule season?"

"'Tis your only choice." Gordon stood. "Or ye could find yourself a comely lass and get married."

"Ye cannae be serious?" demanded Cormac.

"Why not? Ye are the laird and 'tis long past time since ye should have taken a wife, or any woman for that matter. Ye let the last one get married, afore ye had a chance to ask her."

He shuddered. "Nae. I will not get married. Furthermore, Audra and I would not have made a good match."

"Humph! She was a beautiful lass, and your eyes followed her everywhere."

"I can look at beauty. However, the lass was meek and shy."

"Ye might want to make a list of what ye desire in a woman, my laird, and I can have the men search for her," stated Gordon as he walked out of the hall.

Cormac could hear his friend grumbling all the way out of the castle. Standing, he wandered over to the hearth, letting his gaze linger on the flames. Gordon was correct. He should have found a wife many moons ago. Many of his close friends were now happily married, including the MacKays—the Dragon Knights of Urquhart. They had found happiness with these women, and he was truly happy for his friends.

Once, he had longed to have a woman share his life, home, his bed. However, as the years went by, Cormac found fault with those who were presented to him by other chieftains. Worse, he only bedded a woman until she demanded more from him. When that occurred, he sent them packing.

He glanced at the tapestry of his parents. A blessed union, until his mother died. He had then watched his father descend into a dark abyss of drinking and melancholy. His mother's death had ripped the spirit from his father, and he was never the same. Nae, Cormac would not let anyone torment his soul so much as to wish to die. Feelings that powerful were not for him—*ever*.

Gazing back into the flames, he let out a heavy sigh.

****

"How do ye fare?" asked Cormac as he stepped into Moira's chamber. "I brought ye some broth," he said setting the trencher on a nearby table.

"Slop," she protested. "If 'tis the one made by Grizel, then I have nae wish for any."

"I believe Ina prepared this one," he stated, bringing a chair to her bedside.

Moira eyed him skeptically. "Since when does the laird tend to my needs? Fetch one of the others. Ye should not be doing this."

"Aye, I'm laird of Castle Creag, and as such, I am permitted to help any who require my aid. Ye happen to be under my protection." When she started to object further, Cormac held up his hand to stay her words. Sensing her foul mood, he continued, "I am here on another matter."

He lifted the spoon to her lips and waited. She grumbled a curse, but then relented. Cormac dipped the soup back in the trencher. Giving her another mouthful, he asked, "Can ye think of anyone we can send for in the village to help out in the kitchens?"

"My kitchens?"

"Aye. *Your* kitchens."

She puckered her lips in concentration. Slowly, Moira let out a chuckle. "Aye, I do suppose there is one I would let into my kitchens. Though, ye may have a daunting task trying to get the woman here."

"Why? Is the woman in the next village? The snows are not so heavy."

Moira chuckled. "'Tis naught to do with the weather. Her name is Glenna. She keeps to herself. Does not like to be around others. Ye can find her on the other side of Wolf Cavern."

Frustration clawed at Cormac. "Then *why* would ye suggest the woman?"

"Well, ye see, she is the only one I ken who can cook better than me. She can make a fine venison stew to outdo any other. And if ye ken me, Cormac Murray, I accept no one's cooking over mine."

"There is no other ye can think of, Moira?"

"None. Now feed me some more of this broth. 'Tis good, but I warn ye, dinnae tell Ina I said so, or the lass will want to rule the kitchens. One good meal does not make a cook."

Cormac laughed. "Dinnae fear, Moira, your secret is safe with me."

Chapter Two

San Francisco—Present day

"Sift together flour, salt, cinnamon, cloves, allspice, and make a faery wish."

"For the love of the angels!" Eve swiped at a curl that had escaped from her cap for the umpteenth time that morning. "What is wrong with the oven temperature? It keeps fluctuating and my breads are not proofing."

Hearing someone chuckling behind her, Eve glanced over her shoulder at the two women standing in the corner of the kitchen. Sally and Linda—two of the most spiteful people she had ever encountered.

"Perhaps if you paid attention and set it correctly, you wouldn't have this problem," suggested Sally. "Besides, your breads are not worth even entering the contest."

Linda waved Eve off as she moved out of the kitchen. "Give it up, Brannigan."

"Yes, they are," she mumbled, watching them leave.

"Don't mind them, Eve," said Tina, walking toward her. "They're a couple of bi—"

Eve gave her a warning look. "Please don't say the word, my friend."

Tina tapped a finger to her head in thought. "I could always find another word or words."

"I have no doubt." Eve rubbed the bridge of her nose contemplating what to do next.

Tina flicked on the oven light. "Were these your test batches?"

"Yes, thankfully. I'm creating a new type of cinnamon spice bread with pecans." Opening the oven door, she reached for some oven mitts and pulled the breads out. Slamming them down on the counter, she shook her head. "Why are they trying to sabotage my efforts in this contest?"

"Because you pose a threat." Tina inhaled the aroma of the partially baked breads. "Smells divine. Such a shame. I was looking forward to a sample."

Eve looked at her friend incredulously. "You can't be serious. They are two of the best chefs in the city."

Tina narrowed her eyes. "Where did you hear such crap? From them?"

"Well…they did say they had both won awards. In addition, they work at The Golden Gate Tower Restaurant. One of the finest here in San Francisco."

She poked Eve in the arm. "Ha! For all we know they may have worked as dishwashers."

Eve looked at her friend skeptically. "If you recall, they had to audition here at The Blushing Rose Bakery—for Helen, the ultimate queen of baking."

"Just because Helen is the owner doesn't mean she can pick the best. Thankfully, there'll be other judges tomorrow." Tina poked at the bread. "Mind if I take a piece?"

"Seriously? It'll be too soft in the center." Eve leaned against the counter. "Gosh, I don't think I'll be ready by tomorrow." She watched Tina take a knife and slice into the bread. All her hopes were in winning the prize money. Five thousand dollars would be more than enough to fix her car and repair the broken down heater her elderly neighbor needed. Eve had done her best in helping the woman, including offering her a place to stay until it could be repaired. Yet, the woman refused. Therefore, each night Eve brought her a hot meal and asked if she needed any supplies.

"Hey, are you listening to me?"

Eve blinked, focusing on her friend. "Sorry, deep in thoughts."

"These pecans taste like they've been soaking in rum."

"Maple rum," corrected Eve.

"Mmm…delish!" Tina licked her fingers. "You do realize you'll have to be in here early tomorrow morning."

"Yes," she grumbled. "Looks like a three a.m. wake-up call for me. At least it will be quiet."

Tina put an arm around her shoulder. "I wish I could help you."

"Rules are rules." Eve patted her friend's hand. "I still don't know why you didn't enter the contest."

Tina arched a brow. "Because I bake and cook for fun. And if anyone had done to me what those two women did to you, they would have to remove all sharp objects from the kitchen." She pulled another piece of bread from the loaf and popped it into her mouth.

Laughing, Eve started to clean up her area of the kitchen. "Thank goodness Helen shut-down the place for a few days. Can you imagine us all working and trying to cater to the customers?"

"Here, let me help," said Tina between bites of bread. "Hand me the bowls."

"You're a sweetheart," remarked Eve as she wiped down the counters.

"It's payback for everything you've done for me. Let me remind you once again, if you had not persuaded Helen with a taste of my peach and brandy tarts, I don't believe I could have gotten this job." She held out her arms. "One look at my tats and Helen would have closed the door in my face."

Eve giggled. "But they're all *food* related." She lightly touched the tattoo of a rolling pin along the inside of Tina's forearm. "I'll never forget when she did agree to hire you—sight unseen, and then you appeared the next day."

"Her eyes bugged out."

"Her mouth opened in shock, too," added Eve.

Both women burst out laughing.

"A great photo moment lost," snickered Tina.

"But a promise was a promise, and we needed someone like you." Eve picked up a towel and started drying dishes. "Helen was desperate. It was only me and Misty. We couldn't count on her to do anything except take customers to their tables. Even that was beneath her."

Tina let out a groan. "Yikes. Please do not mention Misty's name in my presence. The woman had a crush on me. She followed me everywhere."

"She had a love affair for your baking—your talent, that's all." Eve swatted her friend with the towel. "You could have been kinder."

"I'm not a good teacher. Don't have the patience."

Eve smirked. "You don't with anyone. But one

day, my friend, you will have to learn. You have a lot to offer."

Her friend sighed. "So you keep saying."

Scanning the kitchen one last time, Eve folded the towel and removed her apron. "I'm going to have to pay attention tomorrow. I don't want anything or anyone ruining my chances of winning this contest."

"I'll keep an eye on the pit bulls, Sally and Linda, for you."

Eve embraced her friend. "You're the best. Though, leave your mace in the car."

****

When the sun glinted through the windows of the Blushing Rose Bakery, Eve felt a tremor of unease slither down her back. Telling herself it was simply nerves, she tried to focus on what Helen was saying in her usual shrill voice to the crowd gathered around them. The four judges stood off to the side, each clutching a glass of champagne. There were also six contestants all listening with rapt attention, including her. Although Eve's stomach was already in knots, she wanted to get the introductions over with—so the baking could commence.

Crossing her arms over her chest, she leaned against the wall for support. She'd hardly had any sleep after she returned home last night. Still seething over the debacle caused by Sally and Linda, she'd wound up with a headache the moment her head hit the pillow.

"This is all so exciting," whispered Melinda, one of the contestants. She nudged Eve. "Isn't that Chef Austen from the show, Bake for all Seasons?"

Eve nodded. "I love the show. My favorite was the one she did live in Scotland."

Melinda leaned to the side. "Didn't they film it at a real castle?"

"Yes. It was spectacular," Eve uttered softly. "I have it on tape."

"Gosh, I wish I could remember the name."

"Castle Creag."

Melinda tapped a finger to her chin. "I know exactly what I would do if I won the prize money."

Eve glanced at her friend. "Let me guess. A honeymoon in Scotland?"

Smiling, Melinda added, "With a side trip to Castle Creag. Gosh, Kurt would love to go, too. He's been talking about his own Scottish heritage for years. This would be a perfect gift for him."

"For you, too," added Eve.

"But first, I have to win the contest."

"You're so correct, my friend. I'm making my famous loaves of cinnamon bread and eggnog scones."

Melinda rolled her eyes. "I'm doomed."

Eve covered her mouth to stop the laughter from bubbling forth. Quickly recovering after getting the evil-eyed look from Helen, she stepped closer to her friend and lowered her head. "With what you're planning today, I should be the one believing I have no chance in winning."

Melinda winked. "Let the games begin."

For a brief moment, Eve truly wished Melinda would be the one to win the prize money. Yet, she needed it a bit more than her friend did. As they hugged one another and wished the other good luck, Eve said a silent prayer today would be her day to shine.

While Eve walked to her work area, Linda bumped into her. "Oh, you're still here?"

She held up her wooden spoon. "Damn straight!"

Linda's eyes went wide at Eve's declaration, and she quickly moved away.

"About time you took the lead with snappish comments," replied Tina as she walked up alongside Eve and handed her a steaming cup of tea.

"It simply flew out of my mouth." She took a sip and sighed. "You're a sweetheart. I needed this."

Tina embraced her. "All the best!"

"Thanks. I'm ready." Shooing her away, Eve added, "And keep an eye on the wicked witches."

Tina saluted her and walked away.

When Eve settled into the task of making her first items, the soothing sound of classical music combined with the smells and sounds of baking lured her into a state of bliss. Nothing calmed her nerves more than baking in a kitchen. It was her haven, particularly after the death of her parents and being placed with an elderly aunt when she was ten. Aunt Ginger taught her culinary secrets that had been passed down from generation to generation. Her first memories were of standing on a chair in her aunt's large kitchen and dusting flour onto the cutting board in preparation for rolling out cookies.

Though her aunt had died several years ago, Eve often felt her presence when she was baking. *Watch over me, Aunt Ginger. Guide my hands and thoughts. Let my love infuse the baking as you taught me.*

Humming a familiar tune, Eve blocked out the other contestants and focused on her own tasks, reveling in the feel of the bread in her hands and her own memories.

Hours swiftly flew by and when Eve removed the

last batch of eggnog scones from the oven, she sighed in utter contentment. Plating the scones on a silver tray that belonged to her aunt, Eve set them to the side of her beautifully baked cinnamon breads. With two minutes left, she wiped her hands on her apron and stood back.

Looking around the massive kitchen, she gave a small wave to her friend, Melinda. When the buzzer rang signaling the baking time had ended, she waited for the judges to come to her station. Since Eve was the last one they would visit, this gave her a chance to watch as the judges sampled the other's fare.

Of course, they each gave nods of approval on her two rivals, Linda and Sally, but not overtly and Eve felt hopeful.

As they stood in front of Melinda's table, the judges all started to cough. Helen snapped her fingers at one of the employees to fetch some water. Immediately, her friend uttered an apology, trying her best to explain.

Eve quickly stole a glance at Linda who was snickering and whispering to Sally.

Gritting her teeth, she stormed over to her friend's side. "Is something wrong?"

"This is none of your concern, Eve. Please return to your station," ordered Helen.

Melinda wiped away the tears starting to fall down her cheeks. "Salt," she burst out. "Someone put salt in my sugar canister."

Helen cut her off with a wave of her hand. "You are responsible for bringing in your own items. The rules are clear. The Blushing Rose Bakery would provide all the necessary staple ingredients. We are not to be blamed if you chose to bring in your own sugar."

"It was *vanilla* sugar," argued Melinda.

Eve handed her friend a box of tissues. "Obviously, someone tampered with the sugar."

"I will not have you making false accusations," Helen hissed at Eve. "Again, I must state the rules were very clear. Besides, you could have reached for the salt canister instead of sugar in a misstep."

"How dare you suggest such a thing," said a shocked Eve.

Melinda placed a hand on her arm. "Forget it. It's over. Let it go."

Eve looked at Helen and the other judges. Shaking her head, she turned to embrace Melinda. "I'm sorry."

Regaining her composure, Eve walked back to her station and waited for the judges to move along to the rest of the others before coming to her table. All the time, her heart ached for her friend.

When the judges stood in front of her, Eve sliced the bread for each to sample and stood back. Between nods and smiles, they quickly jotted down their notes. The best nod to her baking came when several asked for seconds and Eve rejoiced, since they had not done so with the others.

Eve watched as the judges retreated to Helen's office to discuss and make a decision. Grabbing a chair, she no sooner sat down when Tina appeared at her side.

"What happened?"

Sighing, Eve pushed aside one of her braids. "Apparently, someone tampered with Melinda's vanilla sugar and added salt."

"Son of a…I swear if one of those wicked witches wins, I'm going to take up knife throwing, and they'll be my first victims."

"It's horrible," mumbled Eve, flicking away the crumbs on her table.

"She really needed this money. Kurt recently lost his job and they had drained their savings for the wedding," Tina added.

"No," gasped Eve, glancing at Melinda. "She never said a word."

The door to Helen's office opened and everyone emerged.

"That's my cue to leave. Keeping my fingers crossed you're the winner." Tina fled to the other side of the room.

Helen cleared her throat. "I would like to thank all my lovely guest judges for honoring The Blushing Rose Bakery's First Annual Bake-Off with their support and time." She turned to Chef Austen. "If you would do the honors of announcing the winner."

Eve stood and held her breath.

"Thank you," stated Chef Austen. "It was a difficult decision, but in the end, most of us agreed that Eve Brannigan's Cinnamon Bread with Pecans and Eggnog Scones were the winner."

The kitchen exploded into a hearty round of applause and shouts—mainly from Tina, but when Eve looked at Melinda, she saw her friend giving her a two thumbs up through her tears.

"Thank you," she managed to say as Chef Austen handed her a trophy and a check for five thousand dollars.

Her smile faltered, as the other judges made their way to congratulate Eve. How could she rejoice when in her heart the win was marred with a tragedy? Linda and Sally had already left, not bothering to clean their area. It was evident they had spoiled Melinda's chances at winning.

Although, it could have been Eve today.

Nodding and smiling at those in passing, Eve made her way to Melinda. "Why didn't you tell me about Kurt?"

Melinda shrugged as she cleaned her table. "Because, my friend, you would have tried to help in some way. You've done so much already with helping us out with our wedding."

"This is not fair. First Kurt loses his job and now this sabotage."

"It will be all right."

"Yes, it will." Reaching into her pocket, Eve slapped the check onto the counter and endorsed it over to Melinda. "Take your trip to Scotland."

Melinda backed away. "I will *not* take your prize money."

"It's my gift to you and Kurt. I was going to use it to get you a fabulous gift and now it's even a better one."

"I...can't," she sobbed. "You need a car."

"No worries. I got the loan the other day," lied Eve.

"That's wonderful, but I still can't accept this generous gift."

Eve placed her hand on her hip. "I just signed it over to you, so please take it." Smiling she added, "At least I won, which was more important."

Melinda brushed her fingers over the check. "We really could use the money," she uttered softly.

"Great, but let's keep it between us."

"I love you, Eve," said Melinda, hugging her fiercely.

"Love you, too," replied Eve.

Giving her friend one more hug, Eve made her way back to her area and started to clean. Yet, her thoughts turned inward to her own predicament of fixing her car and her neighbor's heater.

She took a bite of one of the scones and sighed. "Hmm…perhaps there's another contest I can enter."

Chapter Three

"Weave together the ribbons of time—from the red, green, silver, and gold."

Cormac stood on the North Tower rubbing his hands together to ward off the bone chilling air seeping throughout his body. Snow had fallen heavily during the night, and he grimaced when he made his way to the tower and glimpsed the area covered in a thick blanket of white. There would be no traveling to the village today.

He rubbed at his chin in frustration. The morning meal consisted of blackened bread—once again. Furthermore, Cormac would bet his best sword the evening meal would be the same. If he and his men had to endure one more meal of Ina's vegetable pottage, so thick they had to wash it down with ale, he would take over the kitchens himself. And their precious ale should be savored nae gulped.

"Bloody hell," he hissed. Glancing up at the gray sky, he shook his head. "Hear my plea, Gods of the skies. I ask ye to hold back more snow until I can make it to the village and return. We are heading into dark days here at my home, and I would wish them to be filled without grumblings from my men. Grant me two days to make it past Wolf Cavern and return with a cook."

At the sound of approaching footsteps, he glanced to his right and let out a groan. "By the look on your face, Wallace, I deem ye are here to deliver unfavorable news, aye?"

"Sadly, 'tis true. Trouble in the kitchens again."

"By the hounds of Cuchulainn!" roared Cormac, slamming a hand against the stone wall. "Pray tell it does not involve Ranald and Bran."

The guard's mouth twitched. "Nae, another. Tomas."

"Tomas?" Closing his eyes, he waved his hand outward. "Give me the account."

"The lad fetched a pail of milk as Ina had ordered. Upon returning, he collided with her in the kitchen, spilling the contents everywhere."

Cormac slowly opened his eyes. "Dinnae tell me there was another injury?" *Forgive me but please, Goddess, let it be the lad and not the cook.*

"Ina has done damage to her ankle. She is unable to stand."

"Lugh's balls! Is there a curse over Castle Creag?" He started to pace.

"We will have to tend to our own meals," responded Wallace.

Cormac paused. "Do ye honestly believe I will let the men wander into the kitchens when they feel the need to fill their stomachs?"

His guard rubbed the back of his neck. "Nae. Not a good plan."

"Can the lass tend the fire with help?"

"If she stops wailing, aye."

He sighed. "Is the swelling too much for her to sit?"

Wallace shrugged slightly. "I have not witnessed the lass's ankle."

Bracing his hands on the ledge, Cormac gritted his teeth. The hands of fate were dealt and he must comply. "Send John and Gordon to my chambers, and then bring me news of the lass. If she can manage, and the swelling is light, I can have another assist her."

The guard nodded and departed.

He narrowed his eyes when the first flake of snow landed on his face. "I fear this is going to be a verra long winter."

Quickly leaving the tower, he made his way to his chambers. Upon entering, his wolfhound lying beside the blazing fire, lifted his head and yawned, stretching his long legs.

Cormac bent down near the animal and rubbed his ears. "Fergus, there are times I wish I was a dog. Ye have all the comforts and nae responsibilities. 'Tis a warm fire for a cold day."

Fergus thumped his tail in response.

Standing, Cormac went inside his inner chambers and pulled forth a satchel from the trunk by his bed. Retrieving a small fur wrap, he went back to his study and placed the items on a chair along with his cloak and gloves. When he looked up, John stood at the door.

"Ye sent for me, my laird?"

"Aye, John," replied Cormac, motioning for him to enter. "I have a special task for ye. I am leaving Creag for a few days to travel to one of the villages past Wolf Cavern. Since we have lost another cook, ye are the lone one I can trust to make sure the men are fed, though it will be meager. I dinnae want to return to find the larder empty."

John shifted slightly. "May I inquire how long ye will be gone?"

"Depends on the weather. I am now forced to leave today." His voice grated harshly. "I pray to make the journey in two days."

"God's blood! Only two days?" asked Gordon upon entering Cormac's chambers. "Ye do ken the path is thick with snow?"

Cormac approached his friend and smacked him hard on the back. "Aye, and ye shall be traveling with me."

Gordon let out a curse.

"I knew ye would be pleased." Cormac laughed. "Go make ready the horses, and inform Tiernan to prepare another horse. I dinnae ken if the woman owns one."

"Aye," grumbled Gordon strolling out of the chamber.

"Is there anything else?" inquired John.

Cormac waved him off. "Only a prayer for our safe return."

John smiled. "Done, *my laird*."

No sooner did John leave than Wallace entered. "The lass has stopped wailing, and is settled on the kitchen bench with furs."

Cormac poured ale into two cups, and handed one to Wallace. "No doubt ordering all within hearing."

"Between fits of sobbing," the guard replied. "Is there no way we can persuade Moira to return to the kitchens?"

"Her injuries are more severe." Cormac pointed a finger at the man. "And not one word of this latest skirmish to her."

Wallace gazed at him over the rim of his mug. "Too late."

"The woman has ears everywhere," snapped Cormac. He drank deeply, regret heavy at leaving the warmth and comfort of his home. "Make ready. We leave within the hour. Ye will be coming, as well."

Wallace choked on his ale. "Aye." Wiping his mouth with the back of his hand, he handed the mug back to Cormac.

Setting both mugs down, he gathered his items off the chair, gave Fergus one last ruffle across his head, and walked out of his chambers.

Making his way along the corridor, he paused outside Moira's chamber. The woman was issuing orders in a loud, demanding voice to one of his guards. Cormac shoved a fist against his mouth when he heard the guard let out a groan, which resulted in another barb from the woman. Good, he mused. His men had better learn to heed her demands, or lest she would leave and never return.

"Gods and Goddesses help us on that day," he whispered. Shaking his head, he crept silently down the stairs.

Upon stepping into the kitchens, he saw Ina sobbing quietly as John held her quaking body. The man lifted his head at Cormac's approach.

Cormac raised an eyebrow. *Have ye gone soft for the lass?* He fought the smile forming on his lips.

John shrugged and stepped away.

"If ye are in pain, Ina, ye may retire to your chamber. I have nae wish to make ye suffer," said Cormac.

The lass dabbed at her face with her shawl. "Och,

nae, sir. If Sir John can aid with the meals, I am sure I will make do."

Cormac nodded. "Good. Dinnae forget to heed Moira's counsel, too."

"Aye. Of course."

"If I may have a word with ye, *Sir* John." Cormac motioned to the corridor outside the kitchens.

John coughed into his hand to hide his embarrassment and quickly followed. "Before ye say anything, I never told the lass to call me thus."

Chuckling, Cormac handed his satchel to the man. "I can tell the lass will be well tended to. Since ye are now part of the kitchen staff, fill this with dried meat, cheese, bread, and anything else ye deem we require on our journey. Enough for three. I will await ye in the stables."

"Aye."

When Cormac stepped outside, the cold, brittle air slapped at his face. Refusing to let the elements hinder him, he trudged onward to the stables. When he entered, Wallace and Gordon were standing to the side, each ready to depart.

Tiernan, his stable master, approached. "Ye tempt the Gods by making this journey in foul weather."

"And what would ye suggest?" demanded Cormac taking the reins of his horse.

"Learn to cook."

Hearing the laughter from his two men, Cormac glared at them. Turning his attention back to his stable master, he placed his fists on his hips. "Humph! Ye are always uttering foolish babble."

"The men would surely starve," stated Gordon.

"Or ye would set fire to the kitchens," added

Wallace.

"Exactly my point," agreed Cormac. "Offer your prayers for our safe return."

Tiernan smacked Cormac's horse on the rump. "I shall make ones for the animals, since the weather is a hardship on their bodies."

"Ye wound me," teased Cormac. "I have always been good to Fingal." However, he expected nothing less from the man who loved his horses more than his laird.

"And it won't be the last of my prayers to the animals," protested Tiernan and ambled to the back of the stables.

John soon approached with the satchel. "I added some apples and meat pies."

"Save the apples for the horses," shouted Tiernan.

Cormac secured the satchel on his horse. "Nae fear. I will tend to them myself."

"Safe journey," replied John.

As the men mounted their horses, they slowly made their way through the bailey and gatehouse. The guards nodded at their passing and a settling of unease slipped within Cormac. Crossing the bridge, he glanced over his shoulder at his home.

Gordon approached by his side. "What is it?"

He frowned, unable to account for the man's question. How many times had he ridden out of his home? From battles to visiting friends—it was always the same. He left and returned. Naught changed. Now, Cormac deemed he was standing on the edge of something he could nae fathom and this bothered him. Not prone to visions or such like his good friends, the Dragon Knights, he almost wished for their counsel.

Were the Fae speaking to him? If so, why would they?

Nae. Foolish thoughts. Ye are the one getting soft with age. Aye, that's what Angus MacKay would tell him.

Turning back around, Cormac gave a reassuring smile to Gordon, and waved the man onward.

Yet, with each stride taking them further away from Creag, Cormac could not rid himself of the feeling that something waited for him.

Casting his gaze upward, he sighed. "Watch over our journey, Gods and Goddesses." Touching the silver torc around his neck, he added, "As the Yule draws near, I have always honored the light ye bring. Let ye bring forth a new one, as well."

When a shaft of sunlight pierced through the thick gray clouds, Cormac smiled, knowing the Fae had heard his prayer.

Chapter Four

"Always make sure to leave the Good Folk cookies and milk for the seeds of love they spread on your path."

Climbing the stairs to her apartment building, Eve fumbled for her keys. Though the hour was late, she needed to check in on her neighbor, Mrs. Wilson. The long bus ride home took a toll on her nerves—ones that were already a wreck. She wanted nothing more than to climb into her bed and sleep for days.

Grumbling a curse, she got inside and slammed the door shut on the wet fog. As she made her way to the stairs, she noticed the sign on the elevator. "It's fixed," she uttered in astonishment. No matter how many times she placed a call to the property owner, the blasted thing had remained broken for over a year.

Opening the gate, she slipped inside and pulled it shut. "This better not be a joke." Pushing the button to the fifth floor, Eve held her breath.

In one smooth move, the elevator rose.

"Hallelujah!" she shrieked gleefully. "I will never take you for granted again."

The doors opened silently, and Eve blew a kiss at the contraption before making her way down the hallway. Halting in front of Mrs. Wilson's door, she could hear music playing inside. "Are you listening to

Irish music again?" she uttered softly. Smiling, she knocked on the door.

A beaming Mrs. Wilson greeted Eve. "Come on inside. It's good to see you this evening, but you shouldn't have bothered. I know you had a long day." The older lady led her to one of the oversized chairs. "Let me turn down the music."

Eve slumped down on the soft cushions and dropped her purse. The room smelled of lemon, spices, and yeast, infusing her tired soul.

"Can I get you a cup of tea?" Mrs. Wilson wandered away without giving Eve a chance to reply. "I've been baking all afternoon—from cookies to bread. You'll never guess what happened today."

Suddenly, Eve bolted upright from the chair. "It's warm in your apartment."

"Lovely, isn't it?" shouted Mrs. Wilson from the kitchen.

Eve removed her scarf and went to the radiator. Glorious heat poured out, and she warmed her hands in the warm air. "About bloody time the owner took care of you," she said.

"You mean *new* owners," corrected Mrs. Wilson bringing a tray loaded with plates and goodies. Setting it down on the trunk, she returned to the kitchen.

"Yes! Woohoo!" Eve fist pumped the air, happy with the good news.

Mrs. Wilson strolled back into the room with a steaming pot of tea. "My sentiments, as well."

Eve waited until her friend was settled, then she picked up a lemon cookie. "These are my favorite." Taking a bite, she savored the sugary treat. "I can't believe this all happened today. You must tell me everything."

Pouring tea into their cups, the woman laughed. "Not until you tell me what happened at the contest."

Wiping the crumbs from her face, Eve picked up her cup. "Well…"

"Eve Brannigan, don't keep an old woman waiting."

"I won," she said, smiling over the rim of her cup.

"Bless my soul," gasped Mrs. Wilson. "What a day for wonderful gifts."

"I believe it was my bread, though they really loved the eggnog scones."

"You soaked the pecans like I suggested?"

"Sure did. Enough to coat and then dipped them in sugar." Eve sipped her tea and reached for another cookie.

"They should put your bread on the menu at the bakery," added Mrs. Wilson.

"I'm sure Helen will have something to say about any additional food items."

Mrs. Wilson removed her apron. "That woman doesn't know she has a gem right before her eyes."

"Gem?" asked Eve between bites of her cookie.

"You. The bakery has doubled its business since she hired you."

Eve waved off her praise. "*That* woman purely sees dollars not the people. Now tell me all about the new owners."

Chuckling, Mrs. Wilson refilled Eve's teacup. She settled back in her chair. "Took me by surprise when I heard the knock on my door this morning. There stood the sweetest looking young couple I had ever seen. They made their apologies for intruding so early and announced they were the new owners—Mr. and Mrs. MacNeill. They wanted a list of everything that required fixing. Of course, once I invited them in, you should have heard Ailsa's gasp." Mrs. Wilson reached for a cookie. "She was horrified at the dampness and cold air in my room. The young woman promptly pulled forth a pad and paper and jotted down some notes."

Eve frowned. "And they—Ailsa, and Mr. MacNeill—"

"His name is Kenan." Her neighbor shook her head. "Such a sweet couple."

"How could they manage to get someone out on a Saturday? We were often told repairs could not be done on these older buildings on the weekends."

Mrs. Wilson snickered. "Sounds like lies to me."

"That penny-pinching weasel." Eve pointed a finger at her friend. "I wonder what changed his mind on selling this place. It's prime location."

"Does it matter anymore?" Mrs. Wilson reached for a napkin. "Our days of dealing with Mr. Rogers are done."

"You're right. Good riddance." Eve rubbed a hand over her forehead. "It's amazing what Kenan and Ailsa did in one day. Anything else new?"

"Not from me, but they did say they would greet each tenant," replied Mrs. Wilson. "I'm sure we'll be hearing the praises from others here in the building."

Eve stretched her legs out. "I can hardly wait. I'm thrilled the elevator is working."

"A blessed relief, too! I dreaded climbing those stairs." Her friend put a hand on the teapot. "More?"

"No thanks." Eve leaned forward. "If I stay any

longer, I'll curl up on your sofa and go to sleep. It's so cozy in here."

Mrs. Wilson laughed. "Feel free to do so. There's a blanket to your left."

Standing, Eve grabbed another cookie. "What I need is a hot shower and no alarms on my clock. Simple, blissful sleep." Stuffing her scarf into her purse, she pulled out her keys.

"I'm so proud and happy for you, Eve. Onward and upward to more exciting things. A challenge to seek something else."

Eve smiled. "Thanks. Now that I've won, maybe something will come out of this—say a newspaper article. Nothing grand, but a wee bit of recognition would be nice."

Standing abruptly, Mrs. Wilson grasped Eve's arm. "I completely forgot." Dashing out of the room, she added, "Wait a moment. I have something for you."

"What? Did someone leave me a million dollars?" Eve snatched a gingersnap from the plate, not caring how many she had eaten. It was going to be a wonderful evening with no plans for tomorrow.

Mrs. Wilson rushed back into the room and held up a large envelope. "This arrived shortly before you."

Eve dumped everything back on the sofa and shoved the cookie into her mouth. Taking the item from her, she moaned. "Great cookies."

"I'll pack some up for you."

"Not too many. I'll devour them in one sitting."

"Piff." Her friend waved her off.

As soon as Mrs. Wilson departed, Eve turned the envelope over. Beautifully scripted writing detailed her name on the front. Curious, she broke the wax seal and pulled out an elegant sheet of parchment paper. Her hands trembled as she read the letter.

Congratulations, Eve Brannigan!

As part of our esteemed respect for your success in winning the Sweet and Savory Contest at the Blushing Rose Bakery, we would like to extend the invitation to have you prepare desserts at our annual Winter Solstice Feast at Castle Creag in Scotland. Your transportation will be provided for through Tara Fae Tours. In addition, accommodations will be arranged for you to stay at the Castle located near Inverness.

Enclosed you will find your airline ticket. A limousine shall escort you to the airport in the morning. Please be ready to depart by 5:00am. We hope you will grant us the pleasure of your company, and that you will consider staying until Hogmanay.

Sincerely,

The Clan Murray

"Me? They want me?" she mumbled, as the room spun.

"Goodness, child. Are you all right?" Mrs. Wilson rushed to her side, dropping the container of cookies on the table.

Eve's lip trembled. "They want *me* to bake at a castle in Scotland. Miss Eve Brannigan," she choked out, while pointing a finger at herself. Handing the woman the letter, Eve sank down into the chair.

Mrs. Wilson grinned as she silently read. Afterwards, she embraced Eve. "What an opportunity. And only moments ago we were discussing your future."

"I can't believe it. There must be some mistake," whispered Eve.

"Humph!" Mrs. Wilson retrieved the package and pulled out the ticket voucher. "Here's your ticket, so you'd better get packing."

"But what about work on Monday? I don't expect Helen to give me two weeks off, no matter who these people—"

"Clan Murray," corrected Mrs. Wilson.

Eve raised an eyebrow. "I believe Helen would have harsh words even if it was the Queen of England who sent me the request. She'll never let me go, especially during the holidays."

"What's on the floor?" asked her friend.

Eve bent and picked up another sheet of parchment, though this one was folded. As she opened the note, she burst out laughing. She handed Mrs. Wilson the paper. "It seems everything, including my job, has all been arranged."

"This is wonderful. Now stop fretting and go pack." She gathered Eve's belongings and dumped them into her arms. Placing the container of cookies on top, she literally propelled Eve toward the door.

"But this is all so sudden. I don't have any cash on me. My best clothes are too tight, as you well know at this time of year—holidays and indulging," spouted Eve over her shoulder.

"Stop! You're a stunning lady, and I'm sure there are ATM's at the airport." Opening the door, Mrs. Wilson reached inside Eve's purse and pulled out her keys. Moving her across the hall, she opened Eve's door.

"You're sure a bossy lady," teased Eve.

Mrs. Wilson tossed the keys on a table inside the door. Taking Eve's face in her hands, she said, "Enjoy your trip to Scotland, my friend. I love you. Who knows, you may fall in love with a Highlander."

Eve burst out laughing. "You've been reading too many romance novels."

"They're good for the soul and heart." Giving her a kiss on both cheeks, she strolled back to her door.

"Yeah, right." Eve dropped her purse and hung her coat on the rack to the left of the table.

"I'll leave a book at your door. It's a long flight, so you'll need something to pass the time. Any preference for time period? Modern, Regency, Medieval?"

Eve tried not to roll her eyes at the woman. "You choose one."

Mrs. Wilson blew her a kiss and closed the door.

Shaking her head, Eve closed her own door and leaned against the wood. Of all the dreams she had dreamt, taking a trip to Scotland and baking for a gathering was one she never believed possible.

"Sweet Christmas!" She smacked her palm on her forehead. "Who cares what I'm going to wear. What am I going to *bake*? And for how many? This is a dream come true, but I smell a potential disaster."

Glancing up at the clock, she moaned. It was nine o'clock and all she wanted was to soak in a tub and forget the world existed for a while.

Yet, her nerves tingled with excitement. Moving away, Eve picked up the envelope and headed to the kitchen. Reaching for a bottle of water, she re-read everything. "Of course I'll stay until Hogmanay. Two whole weeks without the harpy Helen. Who cares if I have to prepare desserts for a hundred—heck two hundred. It will be a far, far better place."

Humming a Christmas tune, she ambled to her

desk, pulled out a tablet and pen, and walked into her bedroom. Making a list helped to soothe her and organize the trip—from clothes, toiletries, and making sure no bills were due. She jotted down ideas on what to bake and their recipes, and made a note to include one of her favorite small cookbooks. The long plane trip would be an excellent time to strategize and plan.

Yawning, she stretched and realized an hour had passed. Retrieving her suitcase from the closet, she started to pack. "Scotland in winter. Lovely. Cold. Snow. Horse drawn sleighs. Mistletoe. Scratch mistletoe—only for lovers. Evergreens. Holly. Sugary treats."

She turned at the sound of light tapping. Running down the hall, she opened the door. Clamping a hand over her mouth to stifle the bark of laughter, she shook her head. Lying on the ground were several romance novels wrapped with a plaid ribbon. Picking them up, she felt the heat creep up into her face. The top book depicted a sexy, half-clad Highlander.

Closing her door softly, she was tempted to leave them on the table, but curiosity always got the better of Eve. So carrying them like a prized possession, she marched back into her bedroom and stuffed them into the backpack she was bringing on the plane.

Letting out a sigh, Eve twisted her long curls into a knot on her head and headed into the bathroom. Gazing back at her reflection, she couldn't even remember the last time she went on a date, or had any friendly male conversations. No one sought her out and honestly, she didn't seek out men. They were all self-absorbed with their jobs in the city, or interested in sex for a night. In addition, if she went out with others, Eve was the girl men didn't see.

Turning around, she stomped back over to her backpack.

"I don't have time for love," she stated harshly. Her hand hesitated over the books, as she reconsidered leaving them home. Uncertainty settled within her after she spewed forth the words. Snatching her fingers back, she shook her head.

"Nothing wrong with a little light romance on this trip, as long as it remains within a story."

Chapter Five

"A minstrel's tune played across the snow covered hills until it struck a chord within the heart of the warrior."

Cormac growled and dismounted from his horse. "Please tell me we can cross to the left around the fallen trees?" Since the limbs and trunks bore no fresh snow, he believed the latest problem had happened recently.

Gordon's lips thinned. "The tops hang over the edge of the gully, and the stream is now a flowing river of ice and water. The horses will not be able to pass through."

"Lugh's balls," he hissed. Cormac turned to his right. "Then we must make our way upward over the hill."

"And risk losing one or more of our horses? 'Tis treacherous. Even if we make it over the hill, we will have to venture back around to make our way through Wolf Cavern."

Cormac ignored the man and stepped away. Scanning the area, he searched for the safest path through the trees. It would not be easy, nor was it difficult. The snows had been light in the past few days, and he deemed they all could pass without incident.

"I say we return to Creag. Surely Moira can oversee Ina and the others in the kitchens," suggested

Wallace, reaching for an ale skin off his horse.

"Did I ask for an opinion?" demanded Cormac. "What about Yule? The families who live under my roof and have my protection? Some have lost husbands and fathers during the battles with the evil druid, Lachlan. I made a vow to them that we would celebrate this Yule as a joyous one. Unless ye want to be assisting in the kitchens, which I can order, I reckon this is the wisest solution." He waved his hand toward the right. "The path to the far right of the tree roots is not as steep. We will lead the horses slowly. I have no desire to return to Creag without a cook."

Both showed remorse on their faces and nodded slowly.

"Good. Ye are warriors and used to harsh times, but I will not ask the families under my care to suffer anymore than they should." Cormac moved forward and took a hold of each man. "I chose two of my best men to accompany me, so dinnae say a word about the *treacherous* climb or *losing* a horse. We have battled far worse."

"Ye are correct, as always, my laird," said Gordon. He nodded to Wallace. "My friend is missing the comforts of his ale, furs, and the soft woman who shares it with him."

"Beg pardon, but I recall pulling ye from the bed of *two* women the other morn when ye were absent from the lists," chided Wallace.

Cormac roared and pushed away from them. He grabbed the reins of Fingal while he continued to listen to the bantering between his friends. "Women," he muttered.

It had been many moons since he had bedded a

woman. Aye, there were a few who caught his eye, but after his last battle with Lachlan, Cormac returned home with an ache of something missing. In the beginning, he blamed it on the MacKays and their happy married lives but swiftly discarded the feeling. Instead, he blamed it on the battle that left scars on not only his people, but also his soul.

Did he want more? A wife and family to fill a longing inside? *Nae*. He quickly shoved the thought aside. His family was at Creag. The men, women, and children were his family. He did not need, nor want any woman to tear his heart to shreds. He shuddered visibly recalling how the MacKays came near to losing their own wives. "Nae, not for me." He uttered the words with such force, his horse snorted.

Giving him a reassuring pat, he said softly, "Ye are my family, as well."

As they made their way up the hill, only once did Cormac re-think his plan to find a cook when his horse stumbled into a large snowdrift. However, he said a silent prayer of help to the Gods and Goddesses and soon they were all safely at the top.

Heaving a sigh, he glanced in all directions. The descent was an easy one, but concern filled him. They would surely not make it through Wolf Cavern by nightfall. Rubbing a hand over his face, he feared saying anything to Gordon or Wallace. Keeping his thoughts to himself, he mounted his horse and waved them onward.

The light of day slowly ebbed, but he kept them moving until the first star of the evening appeared. Halting Fingal, he waited until his men approached.

"More trouble?" Gordon placed his hand on his

sword and glanced around.

"Nae, only we are forced to endure a night in the woods. I fear continuing on this path we will come to harm in the night."

"Thank the Gods we have ale to keep us warm." Dismounting from his horse, Gordon added, "Wood will be in short supply for a fire."

Wallace rubbed a hand across his nose. "Then we might want to seek some from whoever is tending a fire."

Cormac sniffed the air. "Aye, ye are correct. There must be a dwelling nearby." Giving a nudge to Fingal, they took off in the direction of the wood smoke.

They did not have to venture far before the misty tendrils could be seen in the distance. Cormac slowed his horse and smiled. "How could I have forgotten?"

"Do ye ken this place?" asked Gordon.

"Aye, though it has been many moons. I visited with Duncan MacKay during our journey to find the druid." He turned toward his friend. "This is the home of the druid, Cathal."

"Praise be to the Gods."

Once they approached, Cormac dismounted. He waved the two men around the cottage. "If I am correct, Cathal has an enclosure for horses. I shall go greet him." He handed the reins of his horse to Wallace, and then removed his satchel.

His steps quickened, but before Cormac had a chance to knock, the door was flung open.

"Welcome, Cormac!" greeted Cathal.

Cormac arched a brow. "Ye were expecting me?"

"Most definitely, as well as your men. I would not expect the Laird of Castle Creag to journey far from his home during foul weather without others."

"The snows were light, and we are on an urgent quest."

Cathal peered over his shoulder. "And your men are tending to the horses in my meager stable?"

"Aye." Cormac chuckled.

Embracing him, Cathal said, "Do come inside."

Stomping his boots to rid them of the snow and slush, Cormac entered the cottage. The warmth of the fire enveloped him along with the hearty smell of stew. His stomach grumbled. Dropping his satchel, he removed his cloak, and draped it over the bench.

"'Tis good I made plenty." The druid dipped a wooden spoon into the kettle. He waved his other hand to the left. "If ye would be so kind, there are extra mugs. How many men did ye bring?"

"Gordon and Wallace," replied Cormac. Retrieving the mugs, he placed them on the long table.

Cathal wiped his mouth and placed the spoon on the shelf above the hearth. Moving toward the table, he swept his hand outward. "Sit." Taking the jug, he poured some wine into the mugs.

"Ye have wine?" asked a bemused Cormac.

"A gift from the MacKays after the final battle."

"I thought ye would have stayed the winter," suggested Cormac and stretched his arm to work out the knot in his shoulder.

"Although Angus desired me to stay, I deemed it was best to return home for a while."

Cormac took a sip of the wine. "Hard to fathom Lachlan is dead and gone. I truly wish I could have been there. Do ye have regrets, because he was your kin?"

"'Twas a battle only the Dragon Knights could fight." Cathal swirled the wine in his mug. "The day my brother killed another in the name of the Dark One was the day he stopped being my kin. I shall speak no further on the matter."

Both men turned at the soft knocking on the door.

"Ye may enter," called out Cathal and stood.

When Wallace and Gordon stepped inside, Cathal ushered them over to the chairs. "Greetings. Did ye find straw and oats in the back of the stable?"

"Aye," replied Gordon. "Thank ye for your kindness."

"Always," stated Cathal. "Help yourselves to the wine. Cormac, ye can help me dish out the stew. I have bread in the cloth on the other table."

Soon they were all settled and the druid raised his head. Holding his arms upward, he said, "Thank ye Mother Danu for the food—for the blessing of the animal. May it nourish our bodies and feed our spirit."

"Thank ye, Mother Danu," responded the men.

Taking his first bite, Cormac closed his eyes, savoring the rich broth and meat. As he continued to eat, an idea occurred. "Ye are most welcome to return to Creag and help in the kitchens, Cathal."

The druid choked on his stew. Shaking his head, he replied, "Ye honor me, but I must decline. My skills are limited, and I fear Moira would also object."

"'Tis a shame," grumbled Gordon.

"Aye," agreed Wallace. "I cannae remember when I have tasted better."

Cathal leaned back in his chair. "Ye spoke of a quest, Cormac. Should I guess?"

Tearing off a piece of bread, Cormac shrugged.

"Only one to bring back a cook."

"Sweet Brigid! What has happened to Moira?" Cathal asked in a shocked tone.

"Mishap in the kitchens involving two lads and some sheep," responded Cormac. "The outcome caused damage to her leg and both arms were burned. Furthermore, the young lass attempting to manage the kitchens also had an accident. So our quest is to venture through Wolf Cavern and find a woman by the name of Glenna." Dipping the bread into the stew, he popped it into his mouth.

Shock soon turned to mirth in Cathal's eyes. "Ye need not go any further. For ye see, Glenna is helping with a birthing not far. She came to me earlier in the day to fetch some herbs."

"By the Gods, good fortune favors us, then!" exclaimed Cormac.

Cathal laughed. "It would seem so, my friend. Though, how did ye come to ken Glenna?"

Cormac wiped his mouth with the back of his hand. "Moira knows the woman. She spoke well of this Glenna and also said she was the only one she could trust."

"Aye, I have heard the same. Although, she does not like to travel far from her home, so ye may find it difficult to convince her to return with ye."

Raising a brow, Cormac reached for the jug of wine. "Moira believes she will come along if we give our account of troubles and her injuries."

Cathal rubbed a hand through his beard. "Family will call her forth."

"They are kin?" he asked, almost dropping the jug.

"Ahh…I see Moira has not told ye." The druid held

out his mug for more wine. "They are distant cousins. Yet, both equally stubborn."

Wallace and Gordon both groaned.

"Well, she trusts the woman enough to send for her," Cormac stated as he poured the wine. "With Yule approaching, I want this celebration of light to be a feast for those under my protection. Lachlan's destruction has ripped across our land. Now is a time of re-building—one of hope and peace."

Cathal sipped his wine. "Ye speak wisely, *Laird* Murray. In the morn, I shall take ye to Glenna. Tonight ye shall stay here. I have extra furs, unless ye object to sleeping on the ground."

"We welcome your shelter," stated Cormac. "I would be honored if ye traveled back with us to Creag and aid with the festivities."

"It will be a privilege." The druid raised his cup. "To peace once again."

"Peace," they all stated in unison as they raised their cups.

Cathal stood. "More stew, my friends?"

Cormac laughed. "Most definitely. 'Tis a fine venison stew."

"I thank ye for the praise."

After the meal ended, Wallace and Gordon sought out their places by the hearth, while Cormac went to check on the horses one last time. The hearty meal and wine did naught to calm the restlessness that had taken hold of him. It wove its way into his body and mind, and he could not fathom the reason.

Giving Fingal one final pat, he stepped outside and glanced up at the night sky. The stars winked down at him, brilliant against the darkness. He leaned against the stable and rubbed his hand across his chest. "I speak of peace for my people, but why can I not claim it? Is there more I must do?"

"Ye seek answers to questions ye already ken."

Cormac placed a hand instinctively over his sword. "By the hounds! Must ye always sneak around?"

The druid shrugged. "Ye are a trained warrior and should have heard my footsteps."

"I was deep in thought," he muttered.

Cathal poked him in the chest. "Ye have been alone far too long, my friend."

"I am not alone," he argued.

"Hmm…there is a difference between being alone and lonely. Find your answers within your heart."

As Cathal walked away, Cormac raked a hand through his hair in frustration. The druid made no sense and only added more questions to his list. "I am *not* lonely."

Yet, his words sounded hollow, leaving him more twisted inside than ever before.

Chapter Six

Inverness, Scotland—Present day

"The Snow Queen wove sprigs of holly and ivy within the woman's hair and presented her with a cloak of velvet rose petals."

Eve surveyed the black vehicle while the man chatted endlessly about the driving rules and the responsibility of returning the car back to him in excellent condition. Glancing down at the booklet in her hand, she flipped through the pages.

"You cannot be serious?" she complained. "The car has a dent in the back, and it's missing one of its side mirrors."

"I must point out the most important mirror is on your driving side." The man adjusted his glasses on his face. "You have no need for another. As for the dent, I have already made a notation in your paperwork."

Waving the booklet in front of his face, she complained, "And how am I supposed to learn all the rules of driving in this country? I've never ventured out of my own state."

The man shrugged. "You are not obligated to rent the vehicle. It was part of the transportation provided for all those traveling to Creag for the event."

Eve shoved the booklet in her bag. "Is there a bus

to Castle Creag?"

"No buses travel to the castle. This is why they offered to pay for a rental car." The man shuffled the paperwork in his hands. "It is a scenic ride to the castle. You should not have any problems with the traffic at this time of the day. The road that leads to the main castle is not often used. It's a back road, so you shouldn't encounter other vehicles unless they are heading to Creag."

"Perhaps a taxi?"

His eyes went wide. "Unless you are ready to pay almost two hundred pounds—"

"Holy moly! Absolutely not!" Tired from the plane ride and growing irritable with each passing minute, Eve asked, "How long will it take to reach the castle?"

He laughed. "Depends on how fast you're driving."

"Trust me. I'll drive like a tortoise."

"Two hours. But if it starts snowing..." He scratched behind his ear and then looked upward. Sniffing the air, he said, "I think you will have a safe journey."

"Wonderful," she muttered. "I'll take the car."

The man beamed. "Good to hear." Handing her the keys and paperwork, he added, "Remember, you'll only be on the A-82 for thirty minutes until you take the side road through the mountains. Slow and steady. Safe journey and good luck."

Eve gave the man a weak smile as she took the keys. Dumping her suitcase onto the passenger side, along with her backpack, she climbed in. Pulling out the booklet, she tried to make sense of some of the signs. Her biggest fear now was getting out of the roundabouts. They terrified her. If she had trouble with the ones in her own state, she shuddered to think of the ones she had to maneuver here.

Sighing deeply, she shoved the booklet back inside her bag. "Think backward, Eve. Everything is the opposite in this country. You can do this." Stretching her shoulders, she started the ignition, and the car lurched forward.

Smacking her hand on the steering wheel, she remembered this was a clutch. Restarting the car, she shifted into first gear and moved slowly out of the parking lot. The man waved at her in passing, and she nodded. Swallowing her fear, Eve made her way onto the main road, saying a silent prayer for the angels to watch over her and the other cars.

Sure enough, within thirty minutes, she spotted a huge sign indicating the turnoff to Castle Creag. Pulling slowly off the main highway, she breathed a sigh of relief. The road narrowed to two lanes—no cars following behind her and none ahead.

Though there was snow on the roadside, the pavement itself was clear, and the sun a welcoming beacon of warmth and light. "You're actually driving in Scotland, Eve. Who would have thought, right?"

As the road twisted, she shifted the gears with ease, savoring the scenic beauty at a leisurely pace. There was no rush to reach the castle. The morning air was crisp and cool. "Bonny Scotland, that's what ye are." She giggled. "Where did that come from?"

Continuing on her journey, time slowed. Peace and contentment filled Eve. Never before had she experienced such bliss. Onward and upward, she traveled the highland road.

Movement caught her eye, and she slowed down.

A hawk soared in lazy circles in the sky. Fascinated, Eve pulled into a side clearing and watched the mighty bird. Turning off the engine, she took out a small package of shortbread cookies. She munched on her treat, and continued to watch the hawk. It dove one final time and disappeared behind the pine trees.

Wiping the crumbs off her shirt, she started the engine. Pulling forward, the car jerked once, and a loud pop followed. Startled, she turned the ignition off. Quickly getting out of the car, Eve groaned. The front left tire had blown. "Really? *Really?*"

Crouching down beside the flat rubber, she couldn't determine what had happened. "And here I was having a glorious morning." Rubbing her hands together, she stood and glanced around. She was a good hour away from the main highway and probably another two on foot to the castle.

"I'm strong, fit—yeah, right. Strong, yes, but you haven't exercised in months."

Determined not to head back, she gathered her backpack and pulled out her suitcase. Defeat was not an option in her book—*ever*. Removing a hat from her bag, she braided her hair loosely and shoved the hat over the mass. Making sure the vehicle was secured, Eve started her trek along the road.

The beauty of Scotland surrounded her, and she relished being outdoors. Squirrels chatted in the trees, on branches dusted with a light blanket of snow. Eve paused when several jumped from limb to limb, snow powder flying everywhere. Smiling, she moved happily onward.

Lost in her own thoughts and her scenic surroundings, she jumped at the sound of bells. Slipping on a patch of slush, that had edged its way onto the pavement, her legs flew out from under her, and she tumbled off the side of the road. The sky and land blurred her vision as she kept on falling down the snow covered hill.

Landing with a smack near a fallen tree, she shook her head. Smarting from the landing, she blinked, trying to take deep calming breaths. "I will *not* panic." Checking herself for any injuries, Eve stood slowly on shaky limbs and looked at her surroundings. Gone were her suitcase, backpack, and hat. The possibility of making it up the steep incline to the road now gone, and a slight tremor of unease settled inside her. She was soaking wet and her teeth started to chatter.

"I'm in trouble," she choked out. Swallowing the fear, she walked around the tree and tried to see if she could locate her items. Hope flared within when she spotted a dirt road ahead. Rubbing her nose, she kept on searching for her belongings. At the sound of bells again, Eve glanced over her shoulder.

Her mouth dropped open in shock. Two horses were pulling a beautifully decorated wagon. A young couple was having a lively conversation on a bench, while the man dangled the reins of the horses. It ambled along the dirt path seemingly without a care in the world.

"Gypsies?" That's all Eve could think of, especially by the look of their peculiar clothing, too. Waving her hands about, she yelled, "Hello! Can you help me?"

All conversation stopped as the couple glanced her way. "Oh my!" stated the woman.

The man immediately jumped down and rushed to

Eve's side with the woman following closely behind him.

He grasped her arms. "Are you all right?"

"I was on my way to Castle Creag when I took a fall from the road above. I seem to have lost all my belongings, too."

"You poor dear," said the woman. "You're soaking wet, too." She wrapped an arm around her waist. "I think I've got something for you to change into."

"But my suitcase and bag," protested Eve. "If those can be found, I could change in your wagon."

The man had already disappeared through the thick pines. Within moments, he shouted, "I believe I've found your belongings."

"Thank goodness," whispered Eve.

"They're floating down the river."

Eve's shoulders slumped. "I think I'll need those clothes."

The woman smiled and led her to the wagon. Upon opening the door, Eve climbed in after her. The interior was as stunning as the outside. Vibrant colors greeted her along with smells of cinnamon and cloves. Herbs hung over the tiny sink, and a small harp stood next to a velvet sofa. A perfect, cozy, traveling home.

"It's lovely," stated Eve.

"We think so," replied the woman heading to the back of the wagon. She bent down by the bed and pulled out a large chest. "Let me see…" She looked over her shoulder at Eve and then back to the chest. "Yes. This will suit you fine. Oh, and you will need a cloak, too."

Eve frowned. "Cloak?"

"Of course." The woman stood and brought forth a

gorgeous piece of material, reminding Eve of the golden leaves of Autumn. She then held up a stunning medieval looking gown. The material was cream-colored with the neck, hem, and borders of the sleeves trimmed in a tapestry of ornamental bands. Again, the colors—green, brown, and gold were reminiscent of fall foliage.

Eve fingered the material. "I can't accept these clothes. Don't you have a pair of pants—jeans and a T-shirt?"

Grinning, the woman shook her head. "My husband and I do not like to wear such clothing."

"Are you performers?" asked Eve.

"Sometimes. Now off with those wet items and into something warmer." She bundled the items into Eve's arms, along with a towel, and led her behind a screen. "I will pack another gown along with some shifts that will go underneath."

"Honestly, I don't need any more gowns. When I get to the castle, I can see if there's a clothing shop nearby." Eve started to peel off the wet clothes. Even her bra was drenched. After drying her body, Eve picked up the damp items and put them into the sink.

"I believe there isn't a shop within a hundred miles of Creag," called out the woman.

"Drats," she muttered. "Then maybe someone can loan me *something*." Stepping into the gown, she pulled it up and was surprised to find it fit.

"Here, let me button the back."

Eve adjusted herself. "I feel naked without a bra."

The woman giggled. "You are a beauty and don't need one."

"I'm going to feel utterly ridiculous entering Castle

Creag looking like some medieval wench."

The woman spun her around. "You are not a wench, so toss the thought aside."

Feeling the heat creep into her face and neck, she nodded. Though the woman looked younger than Eve, she held an authority of someone far wiser. "Thank you."

"You're welcome. Come sit. I'll towel dry your hair."

Sitting in one of the small chairs, Eve closed her eyes as the woman chatted and praised Eve's golden locks.

"There, I believe you'll do." She stood back. "A feast for the eyes."

"Are you preparing me for a ball?" teased Eve.

She winked. "A banquet one will never forget."

A knock on the door prevented Eve from responding to the woman's statement.

The man, who opened the door, whistled. "A vision. May I escort you to the castle?"

"Yes, please. How much further?" asked Eve, stepping down from the wagon.

The couple both laughed. "About five miles around the bend. The castle is on the other side," replied the man.

As the woman wrapped the cloak around Eve, she said, "Your tumble landed you closer to Creag than you expected."

"I don't know if I should be grateful or not. I've lost everything." Reaching for the man's hand as he helped her up onto the bench, she settled herself in the middle.

A twinkle shone in the man's eyes when he spoke,

"Ahh…but you don't know what tomorrow may bring."

Ambling along the road, Eve pondered the man's words. So far, Scotland had been an amazing adventure, though fraught with mini disasters. However, with each of them, something marvelous did come about. She was truly blessed to come upon this couple after her fall. Thankfully, she'd suffered no broken bones, but most likely would have bruises. She shuddered to think what could have happened if they hadn't been traveling this road.

Leaning back against the wagon, she listened to the woman describe the different trees and other foliage. Wild mushrooms were growing along several oak trees, safe from the recent snowfall, and she pointed out the obvious mistletoe.

The man gave a brief history of Castle Creag— starting with the first Murray. The castle so strategically placed, so secluded it had survived the many battles throughout the centuries and actually thrived. His vast knowledge of the area and castle impressed Eve.

By the time they approached the bend, her mind whirled with many facts about the place. Glancing upward, she gasped at the imposing stone fortress. Sunlight danced off the castle, and she shielded her eyes from the glare.

"I am sorry, but we must leave you here. Our travels take us east and we must arrive by nightfall. I pray you don't mind the walk," said the man, snapping Eve out of her thoughts.

"No, not at all. I'm grateful for the rescue, clothing, and ride."

"It is such a lovely day, too," stated the woman. She gave Eve a hug. "Blessings on your journey."

The man helped her down and gave her a hug, as well. "Stay to the path and you will be at Creag in no time. Let the light guide your path always."

"Thank you—both."

Watching as he climbed back up and took the reins, Eve marveled at the strange, but nicest couple she had ever encountered. As the wagon moseyed along, she waved goodbye and then realized they had never mentioned their names. She had to find a way to return the clothing.

"Hey, what are your names?" she shouted.

The woman turned. "I'm called Ailsa and my husband is Kenan. We were honored to meet you, Eve Brannigan."

"It was nice to meet you, too." Smiling Eve turned around but froze in her steps. How in the heck did they know *her* name? Not once did she mention it. And why did their names sound familiar?

Eve let out a gasp. "Impossible!" She spun around and blinked in confusion. They were gone. Vanished into thin air.

Rubbing a shaky hand across her forehead, she burst out laughing. When her fit subsided, she turned back toward the castle. "What are the chances of me bumping into another couple with the same names as the new owners of my apartment building?"

She kicked a stone out of the way. "Preposterous."

Chapter Seven

"Sugar and spice and everything nice…that's what beautiful maidens are made of."

Clenching his jaw so tight he feared it might snap, Cormac tried his best to remain silent. From the moment they had met Glenna, the woman talked or complained endlessly about everything. She was furious when Cormac approached her in the morn, pleading his best for help with the Yule feast. She scoffed at him and demanded he and his men leave at once, until she saw Cathal leaning on his staff behind them. With the druid's gentle urging and stating Moira could use her skills, she finally relented.

Yet, she grumbled about the weather, not being able to retrieve her basket of herbs, lack of clothing, and anything else that tempted her to give a foul opinion. If he had known the woman's disposition, Cormac would not have sought her out. Nae, he was tempted to dump her off the horse and tend to the kitchens himself.

"I demand ye stop," she yelled behind him.

Cormac glanced over his shoulder and saw the sour expressions on his men. "Why, pray tell?"

"To gather the mushrooms at the base of a tree." Dismounting, she pointed a finger to Gordon. "Hand me a blanket or cloth to bundle them up in."

Gordon rolled his eyes but removed a cloth, which held a small piece of hard cheese. Tossing it to her, he nibbled on the food.

She made some gruff comment as she ambled off to gather the mushrooms.

"God's teeth," grumbled Wallace coming alongside Cormac. "I fear our meals will be tainted. For all we ken, she could be picking poisonous mushrooms."

Cathal chuckled behind him. "Glenna's cooking is known throughout the area. As is her healing ability."

"Can she not keep her tongue silent?" demanded Cormac. "The woman finds fault with the verra air she breathes."

Mirth shone in the druid's eyes. "Ye must learn to bite back. Remember, ye are *Laird* Murray."

Cormac raked a hand through his hair. "I daresay she gives no care to titles or who is laird."

"Ye have faced worse, my friend."

"Humph! She is returning."

"Then, thank the Gods we are nearing Creag. Can ye fathom if ye had to cross through Wolf Cavern with her?"

Cathal moved away before Cormac could respond. Giving a nudge to his horse, he gestured them onward.

He welcomed the morning sun, allowing the warmth to fill his body. His thoughts returned to home, and a prickling of unease skittered across his senses. As he came around the bend in the road, he jerked hard on the reins of Fingal. His mouth gaped open at the sight before him. A woman stood in the middle of the road. She was a vision as the sunlight danced all around her, creating a golden halo of light. His heart pounded within his chest, and he found it difficult to draw breath. Her beauty undid him.

"Sweet Brigid! Surely an angel," stated a stunned Gordon.

Swallowing, Cormac shook his head to rid himself of the image, but she remained standing in their path. "I dinnae believe in angels," he spoke, his tone more gruff than he intended. The lass angled her head to the side and frowned.

"A Fae?"

Cormac ignored his friend and dismounted. "Who are ye?"

She took a few steps backward. "I'm…umm…Eve. Eve Brannigan. Who are you?"

"An English woman," spat out Wallace.

Cormac held up his hand to silence the man. He stepped closer. "Why are ye traveling the road alone? Where is your horse? Your guards?"

"Guards? Why on earth would I need any guards?" She snorted. "A horse? Really? If you must know, I lost everything when I took a fall off the main road. Thank God a couple found me—"

Finding it difficult to follow her words, he held up his hand. "One does not venture onto *my* land without *my* knowledge and surely not a lass walking alone. I have no dealings with the Brannigans and dinnae ken the clan."

Fury shown in her eyes, and she met his stare. "I don't know who the heck you are, but I was invited by the Clan Murray to help with the Yule feast."

Cormac folded his arms across his chest. "Truly ye jest?"

"What is wrong with you?" She peered over his

shoulder. "Why are you traveling on horses? Is it because the road is too narrow for cars?"

Again, Cormac took another step toward the lass. She brushed back a mass of golden curls, and his fingers twitched, longing to touch them. Clenching both hands by his side, he replied, "To travel by horse is more sensible than by foot. If ye were invited, I would ken."

"Why is that?" she countered. "Are you someone special?" She looked him over and shook her head. "No one said we had to dress in medieval garb for the occasion."

Hearing his men snickering behind him, Cormac let out a growl. "I would *ken*, because I am Laird Murray of the *Clan Murray*."

The lass's eyes went wide. "Oh. Sorry." She bit her lip and rubbed a hand over her forehead. "I was invited, honestly."

Whoever the lass was, Cormac was not about to leave her wandering the hills by herself. If she was English, it would be far wiser to have her remain close. Furthermore, he wanted to find out her true purpose for being here.

"Oh, for the love of Mother Danu, just bring her along," protested Glenna.

"Ye say ye were sent to help with the Yule feast? For what reasons?"

She lifted her chin. "I assume it was to help with the baking."

Cormac glanced at Gordon and raised a brow. "Surely not Fae."

"Fae as in *faery*?" She burst out in laughter, and Cormac thought her voice was the most beautiful melody he had ever heard.

When he recovered, he whistled for his horse. The animal trotted aimlessly to his side. Taking her elbow, he saw her flinch. "Would ye prefer to walk up the steep path to the castle? Or ride?"

Again, she bit her bottom lip. "I don't know how to ride a horse."

"Truly?"

She waved him off. "I'm not scared of the animals. I've never had the opportunity to learn."

"Interesting," muttered Gordon.

Cormac smiled. "Dinnae fear. Ye shall ride with me."

Giving her no time to protest, he grabbed her around the waist and hauled her up onto Fingal. When he mounted his horse and settled behind her, Cormac felt her body stiffen as he placed an arm around her waist. He leaned next to her ear. Her mass of curls brushed his face, and he inhaled her scent—one of different spices. Lust instantly surged forth, powerful and intense. "Relax," he urged in a hoarse voice. Though he found it difficult to do so himself.

He felt her tremble, but she nodded. Giving a tug on the reins, they moved up the path.

With each steady trot, her body swayed and Cormac tried to focus on the *road. The castle. Fighting in the lists. Bathing in the icy waters of the loch.* Anything but the soft curves of the lass's body pressing against his own. What was wrong with him? He prided himself on being a man always in control of his emotions—especially his lustful ones. Yet, now he found himself confused, tongue-tied, and his gut twisted into knots.

So deep in his thoughts, he did not notice Fingal veering off the main road until the lass let out a giggle. She had the most musical sound, and he found himself smiling. Guiding his horse back to the path, he could hear his men doing their best to contain themselves. A glance back confirmed William was coughing loudly and Gordon trying his best not to fall off his horse.

"I swear Fingal, I am tempted to trade ye in for another horse. Ye must be going blind, or worse, old."

His horse let out a large snort.

Eve clicked her tongue in disapproval. "For shame, Mr. Murray. How cruel. I think he's a kind animal. Perhaps it's the man holding the reins who can't see clearly the path in front of him?"

The lass was quick with the wit, he mused. "I dinnae ken your word, but ye may call me Cormac." He leaned near her again. "And I can assure ye, I am nae blind, nor old."

She twisted around to look at him, and all he could think of was kissing those full lips. They reminded him of tart berries on a summer day, and he pondered how sweet they would taste.

"You're a strange man, Cormac," she uttered softly.

He shrugged, and she turned back around. "Where is your home?"

"San Francisco. I won this trip, and I'm honored to be a part of your celebrations. Your castle is stunning from the distance."

"I dinnae ken the place. Is it in England?" He grew troubled by her strange words.

Again, she laughed. "No. I wish. It's in the state of California. I'm from America."

Puzzled, Cormac tried to recall if he had heard of the foreign place. She continued to babble on about her home and then burst out in glee at some deer ambling along through the trees.

"Have ye never seen deer?" he asked in astonishment.

"Of course, but not like this. They're stunning! You are fortunate to be surrounded by beauty. Where I live there is constant noises, especially from cars and trains. At times, it can be overwhelming. That's when I retreat to the ocean."

Cormac's mind whirled trying to keep up with what she was talking about. "How does one win a *trip*?"

Eve shifted in an attempt to look at him, and Cormac let out a groan. "Oh, I'm sorry. Did I hurt you?"

Only in a part that craves to be inside ye. "Nae. Ye dinnae have to look at me to answer."

"I'm stunned. I assumed since you are the laird you would know." She shrugged dismissively. "Maybe your staff hasn't informed you. I won the contest at the Blushing Rose Bakery. This was part of my winnings. To bake for the Yule feast here at Castle Creag."

"Ye did come at a grand time. We are in need of help in the kitchens."

She let out a nervous giggle. "Excellent. I was afraid you weren't going to let me inside."

"I do not turn away strangers, particularly women," he stated.

Making their way steadily upward, toward the bridge and Castle Creag, Cormac considered all the words the lass had spoken. As soon as they were inside, he was going to pull forth his maps and have her show him exactly where she hailed from.

Eve gasped. "Spectacular! It looks positively medieval."

Smiling, he shook his head. Cormac thought her daft, but if the lass could cook, he gave no care to her way of looking at everything—*or* speaking. He raised his hand in greeting, and the guard on the North Tower saluted back. A mere moment later, Fergus came barreling through the gate and across the bridge.

"Great Gatsby! Is that your dog? A wolfhound, right?"

"Aye." Dismounting from his horse, he greeted Fergus. The animal turned and sniffed at Eve's feet.

Eve smiled, transforming her entire face. All Cormac could do was stare at the lass, ignoring his own men when they passed by him. "You are a handsome fellow. What's your name?" Her fingers reached down and grazed across his head.

She lifted her gaze to Cormac, and his mouth became dry, unable to answer her question.

"His name is Fergus," commented Gordon. "I believe our laird had a fleeting lapse of thought."

Cormac turned and seeing the smirk on his man's face, he glared at him. *Ye shall pay for that remark in the list.* Reaching for his horse's reins, he led them across the gate and through the portcullis.

Upon entering the bailey, Cormac reached for Eve. She placed her hands on his shoulders, and as she slipped down, their gazes locked. A blush stained her cheek and neck, and he was curious if the rosy glow extended to her full breasts.

"You can release me," she uttered softly.

Cormac took a step back. He clenched his shaking hands and abruptly turned around. Still seeing the smirk on Gordon's face, he ordered, "Ye can take my horse to the stables. I will show Eve and Glenna to the kitchens."

"Are ye sure ye would not rather have me tend to the women?" countered the man as Eve strolled toward them.

By the hounds! His friend was trying his patience. "I believe I gave ye an order," he gritted out.

"Aye, ye did." Gordon winked at Eve and took the reins of the horse.

Turning on his heels, Cormac strode into the castle. Silence greeted him. As of late, the place had been in utter chaos. Now, not one child scampered about. No shouting, wailing, or even a curse flung out. Blissful, peaceful, calm.

His steps quickened. Entering the kitchens, he let out a groan. Seated on a bench was Moira giving strict orders to John on the proper procedure of rolling out bread. Cormac glanced around. Ina was nowhere in sight.

"Where is Ina?" he demanded. "And why are ye downstairs, Moira?"

Moira glanced up. "'Tis good to see ye have returned. The snows were not light." She angled her head. "Unless my eyes deceive me, this is nae Glenna."

"I am right here," snapped Glenna. She moved around Cormac and Eve. "Sweet Mother Danu. Why are ye down here?"

"Whist. I am much better." Smiling, the women embraced each other.

"I am waiting for an account, Moira," stated

Cormac.

The woman snorted. "Naught was getting done. I deemed it far better to remove Ina until she had healed and another could help in the kitchens."

Cormac narrowed his eyes and cast his gaze to John, who refused to meet his hard stare. His temper quickly rising, he said, "I ask for ye to help the lass, not try and bed her in the kitchens."

Eve let out a gasp and all eyes turned to her. "I hope you're going to fire him."

Confused, Cormac asked, "Why would I put fire on the man?"

"Obviously, he tried to take advantage of the girl and should be punished. And that's not what I meant. Sack him. Dismiss the scoundrel and make sure he never returns."

Dizzy from trying to follow Eve's flow of words, Cormac rubbed a hand over his brow. "John is one of my most trusted guards—"

"I love the lass," blurted out John.

Cormac glared at the man.

"My pardon," John uttered quickly.

Turning his gaze once more to Eve, he continued, "As I was saying, John is a guard here at Creag. Trustworthy, loyal, and apparently smitten with the lass."

"Oh. Sorry. But you looked extremely angry at the man." She bit her lower lip and shrugged.

Moira laughed. "Goodness, she sounds like the others."

"Others?" he asked, fearing he would not like her answer.

"Aye, most definitely. She speaks like Brigid and

Deirdre. Where did ye find her?"

Cormac's mind whirled. *Nae! Impossible!* Those women traveled the veil of ages to help Duncan and Angus MacKay with their quest with redemption, along with the other two MacKay brothers' wives—Aileen and Fiona. And then he recalled where Brigid told him she hailed from—a place called America.

Startled by the revelation, Cormac staggered away from Eve Brannigan.

Chapter Eight

"Pluck the petals from the flower, mix with a drop of honey, add a splash of tears, and give to your lover on Yule."

The man was a lunatic. No doubt about it, considering the way he was gaping at her. Eve glanced down at her gown. Was there something horrible attached to the material? Did she step into horse dung?

Yet, each time she peered into his blue eyes, she couldn't look away. She'd never known a man to have such mesmerizing eyes. His blond hair had streaks of gold, as if the sun had painted its light throughout. Usually, Eve didn't like men with long hair. Nope, she preferred her men clean cut and shaven. However, the moment this man stepped into her path, she couldn't stop staring at him. Her breathing became shallow and the air thick. Eve thought a Celtic God had appeared out of thin air.

Yes, Cormac Murray didn't appear to be any ordinary man. A handsome hunk with thick, golden hair that touched his shoulders, add in the shadow of a beard on his face, and her knees went weak.

He reminded her of the hero from the romance story she read on the plane. *Stop! He's nothing more than a man who likes to bark out orders. Yes, he's gorgeous as sin, but don't let his looks fool you.*

Growing weary of his stony expression, she fisted her hands on her hips. "What is wrong now?"

He gave her no time to react before he grabbed her arm and led her out of the kitchens. Stunned, Eve started to protest, but the warning look he gave her would singe the hair off any human being or animal. *Raving idiot!* She clenched her jaw, trying to maintain her composure and not let her fury explode.

Leading her up the stone steps, flames flickered from their holders. Strange, why would they use fire inside the castle for lighting? To make the guests feel part of the medieval atmosphere? Trying to keep up with him, her steps faltered, and she slammed against him. They both landed against a large wooden door.

His grip was tight around her waist, his fingers moving slightly upward. She trembled from his touch, and gazed into eyes that blazed with anger and then changed to confusion.

Releasing her, he glanced around as if he didn't want anyone to see them in the corridor. "My pardons. Ye claim to come from *America*, aye?"

"Yes," she answered slowly, letting her anger settle to a simmer.

"Ye may think me daft—"

"Definitely," she interrupted.

Cormac closed his eyes. "What is the year?"

Why do I always find the bizarre ones attractive? "When I woke this morning, which was on the plane, I believe the year was the same—2016."

Letting out a curse, he moved away from her and started to pace along the corridor. *Someone call for the men in the white jackets.* Slowly edging away from him, Eve turned and fled back down the stairs.

Running into the kitchens, she halted when all talking ceased. "Is there a telephone I can use? I'd like to leave."

"Och, lass. Come here." Moira patted her hand on the bench. "Tell me your name and why ye wish to leave."

Eve snorted and shook her head. Making her way to the woman, she slumped down on the bench beside her. "My name is Eve Brannigan, and I have no desire to be around a maniac. You can all find someone else, but I didn't sign up to be harassed and snapped at."

The woman coughed into her hand, yet, Eve could see she was trying her best not to laugh. "I dinnae ken all your words, but ye must understand our laird is usually good-tempered and a kind man."

"Are you sure we're speaking of the same man?" scoffed Eve. "I was excited to accept the Murray's invitation in the beginning. However, from the moment I arrived in Scotland, there has been one problem after the next. I'm tired, hungry, and have no patience for pig-headed men who do nothing but bark out orders." *Even if you are gorgeous eye candy, Cormac Murray.*

One of the men moved forward. "Greetings, Eve. My name is Gordon. Moira is correct. Our laird has been under strain of late." He placed a gentle hand on her shoulder. "Let me go speak with him. Surely, ye can see we are in need of some aid. The Yule feast approaches and 'tis an important time within our clan. Our men, women, and children have been through trying times."

Eve was sure she was going to regret her decision, but with all the pleading how could she up and leave. "All right, I'll stay, but please keep that man away from me with his foul mood."

Moira sighed. "Thank ye."

"I agree with the lass," stated Glenna. "The Murray is not welcome in the kitchens. Only those we deem can help may enter."

Gordon smirked. "I will inform the laird." He glanced back down at Eve. "I thank ye." Giving her a short bow, he left the kitchens.

"Ye can take your leave, as well, John," ordered Glenna.

"Happily," stated John. Wiping his hands on a cloth, he too quickly left.

Glenna clucked her tongue in disapproval of the kitchens, looking in all directions. "What a mess."

Standing, Eve removed her cloak. "Is there an apron I can borrow? Or better yet, I would love to change out of this gown and into something else. Since I've lost everything, I'll need to make some calls to stores, or do you think someone would be kind enough to lend me some of their clothes. A pair of pants and T-shirt would be fine."

Both women looked at her as if they didn't understand a word she uttered. She was about to re-think her plans on staying when Glenna spoke.

"Fae meddling," she muttered, sweeping aside her long braid.

"Fae," sputtered Eve.

Moira chuckled loudly. "When was the last time ye had a meal, Eve?"

Her question caught Eve off guard. Instantly, her stomach protested, and she grimaced. Confused by the time difference, she shook her head. "A long time. Dinner last night on the plane and a light breakfast.

What time is it?"

"Past midday," replied Moira.

Looking at her wrist, Eve recalled how she lost everything, including her watch. "Don't you have a clock?"

"Sit, lass," instructed Glenna. "Ye shall have a meal, drink, and rest."

Horrified, Eve responded, "Absolutely not. You need my help. I'll snack on something later."

Moira reached for Eve's hand with a pleading look in her eyes. "Dinnae argue with Glenna. Her fury is greater than the Murray's."

Eve complied and sat. She looked at Glenna, who now huddled over the cauldron. "What's cooking?"

"Some slop of cabbage, leeks, and parts I have no wish to mention."

Eve swallowed. "I'm happy with bread and cheese."

"Shh…ye need a proper meal," said Moira softly.

Glenna glanced over her shoulder. "Who helps in the kitchen with errands?"

"There's Nola, Grizel, and when the lad is nae causing mischief, 'tis Tomas."

Striding to the entrance, Glenna shouted, "Fetch me Tomas, Grizel, and Nola!"

Going to one of the work tables, Glenna looked inside the baskets. "Eggs, wild onions, more cabbage—"

"I would be happy with fried eggs, onions, and some cheese," Eve blurted out.

Glenna's brow furrowed in obvious displeasure of the interruption.

"I would be more than happy to prepare my own

meal." Eve smiled, hoping to disarm the woman's displeasure.

Reaching for an apron, Glenna tossed it to Eve. "Let me see what ye can do."

Smiling, she pulled the apron over her head and quickly tied it in place. Stepping to the table, she pulled out a couple of eggs, and onions. Seeing other baskets, she peeked in all of those, pulling out mushrooms and fresh dill. Uncovering a mound of cloth on the table, she smiled at the sight of a large round of cheese. "Where can I chop these items?"

Glenna handed her a large blade. "At the table by the herbs."

"Gotcha." Eve twirled around and spotted the area. Herbs hung drying on beams above a large wooden table. Taking the knife from Glenna, she made her way to the table. "I'm curious, Moira. Why are there not any ovens? With a place this grand, why do you not have the kitchens modernized? Is it all in keeping with the medieval theme?" she asked while chopping the onions.

"There is an oven for baking breads to the side of the hearth. Ye may find it a wee bit different here," responded Moira.

Why was it, no one fully answered Eve's questions? Did they not understand her? "Positively ancient and I'm expected to bake under these conditions?" she muttered. Eve brushed off the dirt from the mushrooms and sliced them. Still pondering over her situation, she considered this a test of her skills. Eve never walked away from a challenge, and she definitely believed this was the most insane one she'd ever encountered.

Placing the items in an empty basket, she moved to

the hearth. "Wonderful," she muttered, realizing there was a good chance she could catch her clothes or the kitchen on fire. Seeing a pan with a long, curved handle, Eve pulled it off the hook. Placing the pan on the iron grate, she tapped her finger to her mouth in thought. "Do you have butter or another form of fat?"

Glenna handed her a small earthenware container.

Lifting the lid, Eve didn't want to know where the fat came from. She scooped out a small portion with her knife, before almost shoving it back to the woman. Going to work on her meal, she wished she had her camera to take a picture of herself cooking in this fashion. The aroma of onions and mushrooms filled the room, and she sighed. Cracking the eggs into the mixture, she reached for a large wooden spoon and scrambled them within the pan. "Any salt?" she called out over her shoulder.

"Ye would dare to use from the salt cellar? 'Tis costly and for the meat and fish. I keep it in the other part of the kitchen." Moira's tone was one of shock.

Good grief! "I only require a pinch, but if you're in short supply, I'll use the cheese and pepper."

"Ye will find the pepper in the spice box. Here is the key."

Eve turned around slowly. "A key…to the spices?"

Moira nodded. "Most definitely." She removed a long black cord with a large key.

"On second thought, I'll stick with the cheese and dill." Shaking her head in confusion, Eve turned back to her cooking. Crumbling up bits of cheese into the pan, she let it melt down. Content with the results, she glanced around for a plate.

Glenna handed her a small wooden one.

Eve scooped out the savory meal and went to sit across from Moira. Both women looked at her meal as if it contained some kind of unearthly specimen. "Any forks?" she asked.

Again, Glenna handed her a rather large item resembling a pitchfork. "Uh…no thanks." Instead, Eve cut a slice of the bread on the table. Digging into her meal, she closed her eyes and savored the flavors. "Mmm…"

Glenna burst out in laughter and poured her something to drink. "Ye can wash down your eggs with ale." She then glanced at Moira. "She will do."

Eve was about to ask what she meant, when three children came running into the kitchen. Presuming them to be the ones Glenna asked for, she smiled at them.

Glenna clapped her hands. "There will be nae running into the kitchens at any time. Do ye understand?"

"Aye," they all responded at once.

Eve hid her smile over the rim of her cup. As she took a sip, she almost choked on the ale. "This is ale?" she sputtered, trying to catch her breath.

"The finest," stated Moira.

Tastes like stale bread. "Is there any water?"

"I can fetch some for ye," replied the lad.

"I would be most grateful. What's your name?" Eve took a small bite of bread.

"Tomas."

"Thank you."

Smiling, he started to dash off, but caught himself and wandered casually out of the kitchen.

The two girls crowded around Eve. "Ye are verra pretty. Are ye here to help Moira?"

"Why, thank you. Yes, you could say I'm here to help Moira and Glenna, as well. What are your names?"

The fair-haired girl answered, "I am Grizel."

"I am Nola," responded the other who had shocking red hair.

"It's a pleasure to meet you both."

The girls giggled.

"Now that ye have made your greetings, I need some fresh milk and fennel from the garden," ordered Glenna.

Both girls sprinted away, hand in hand.

"No running!" yelled Glenna.

Soon Tomas returned with a large jug of water. Setting it down on the table, some of the contents splashed over the sides. "'Tis verra cold."

"Don't worry. I like it chilled." Eve glanced around for another cup, but Glenna pried the one from her hands and dumped the remaining ale back into the jug. Eve nodded her thanks when Glenna handed back the cup.

After filling her cup she drank deeply, relishing the cold water.

"Come with me Tomas. I want to inspect the rest of the meat larder," ordered Glenna.

As Eve watched the two, she continued eating her meal, aware of Moira watching her every move.

Moira leaned forward. "'Tis not what ye foresaw when ye stepped through the gates of Castle Creag?"

Eve wiped away the crumbs from her mouth. "Honestly, no. But I'm here now and willing to do my best."

Reaching her hand across the table, Moira placed it over Eve's. "Cormac Murray is a good man. He has battled many demons, but his loyalty has always been to his clan. Dinnae let his bark frighten ye. When men are scared of their own feelings, they tend to act like stubborn lads."

Curious, Eve asked, "Why are you sharing this with me? It's not like I'm staying any great length of time."

Moira shrugged and pulled the shawl more closely around her body. "Only wisdom to see ye through."

Suddenly, the weight of the past few days took their toll on Eve. Standing she said, "If you don't mind, I'll clean up and then I would like to see my room."

Moira waved her off. "Nae. Another will scour and wash. Knowing my cousin, she will most likely want to do it herself before she prepares the next meal. I believe Cormac told one of the lasses to prepare a chamber. Ye are an honored guest."

"I'm no one special. Any room with a soft bed will do," protested Eve as she started to move away.

"Wrong. Ye may be here to help Moira, but ye are my guest," argued the low male voice, his soft burr sending a tingling sensation across Eve's skin.

Slowly, Eve turned and their gazes locked. Cormac leaned against the wall, his arms behind his back. How long had he been standing there? Heat flooded her face, but she refused to look away. Her breathing became shallow, and her heart lurched when he pushed away from the wall—making his way toward Eve.

She swallowed, hard. The closer he came, the more she had to angle her head up to meet his stare. Neither took their eyes off the other, and as he approached, he held out his hand.

"If ye will permit me, I will show ye to your

chamber."

As she took his hand, the contact of his fingers sliding over hers was electrifying. She let out a slight gasp and noticed he had felt the same. His eyes widened, and then he smiled, leading her out of the kitchen.

Making their way up the narrow stairs, they continued to climb in silence. Walking along a short corridor, Cormac paused in front of a door.

He leaned in close. "I may be stubborn, Eve Brannigan, but I am nae a lad." Opening the door, he bowed slightly. "Sleep well, lass."

Eve watched Cormac walk away. Letting out a long held breath, she knew in her heart sleep would not come anytime soon. Her body and mind were consumed with only one thought—what would it be like to kiss Laird Cormac Murray?

Chapter Nine

"The maiden presented the knight with a gift of her heart, wrapped in gold, silver, crimson, and green."

"Good dog," he muttered softly. Leaning against the window arch, Cormac watched Fergus trail after Eve. From the first day, the dog had attached himself to her—companion and protector, following her everywhere. When one of the guards got too close, the animal let out a short bark of disapproval and stood in front of her. Cormac had rewarded Fergus that same night with a huge bone.

It would seem Fergus was not the only one enchanted by the lass. The entire castle had fallen under her charm. She had taken to the kitchens as if she belonged there, and shockingly, Moira and Glenna—harpy of the north had praised her baking. Not once had he heard a grievance against Eve.

When he had escorted her to her chambers several days ago, he vowed to stay away from Eve. However, her radiance, smile, and voice drew him to her, and often, Cormac would find himself standing outside the kitchens simply for a glance of the lass. She was a siren calling out to him, bringing the lustful beast forth, and something else. Something he preferred not to think about. Had he not made a pledge to never take a wife? *Aye!* Yet, he found his heart softening to the idea.

A lone pig sauntered into the bailey after making an escape from its stall. Eve's laughter drifted up to him as one of the lads attempted to catch the animal—both landing in a snow pile by the gates.

He pounded the wall. "Why did ye send her here, Fae? To tempt and torment me? She is not of this world. 'Tis cruel." Cormac's mind battled his body.

"Bed the lass and end this," grumbled Gordon behind him.

Cormac stiffened at his friend's remark. Glancing over his shoulder, he gave him a cold stare. "Why are ye here?"

Holding up a piece of rotted wood, he replied, "Ye ordered me to see to the blacksmith's door. Told me ye were gathering fresh wood."

"I was on my way," he shot back. "Could ye not wait?"

"For how long? 'Tis midday and ye departed early morn," argued Gordon.

Ignoring his friend's outburst, he pushed away from the wall and strode out the door. "Are ye coming?" he demanded. His steps quickened as he made his way out of the castle. The cold blast of air doused the fire of anger and lust, and Cormac welcomed the embrace.

Entering the stables, he pointed to a cart. "There is your wood. Do ye require anything else?"

"Not at the moment."

"Good."

Storming out of the stables, Cormac collided with the source of his recent fixation—Eve. Grabbing both her arms, he tried to steady them, but managed to twist and fall backwards into the snow. She landed on top of him. Cormac closed his eyes and let out a faint, desperate groan.

"Did I hurt you?" she asked softly.

When he opened his eyes, Cormac gazed into a sea of green. Her eyes held his and he became even more captivated. He lifted his hand, and gently brushed the curls from her face. He felt her tremble from his touch. "I am nae hurt. And ye?"

"No."

Inhaling her scent, he said, "Ye smell of cinnamon."

A rosy stain spread across her cheeks. "I'm attempting to bake cinnamon bread, but I don't believe it will do well. I need more sugar."

Cormac was sorely tempted to steal a kiss from the lass. Would her lips taste of sugar? Before he could find out, Fergus interrupted the moment—when he ambled over and licked Cormac's face.

Eve burst out laughing and rolled to the side and stood up.

"Off with ye. Your breath is foul smelling." He shoved the dog away in a playful gesture and stood also. Brushing the snow off his clothes, he did the same to Eve's back.

"Ye do ken sugar is like gold here—more so in the winter. Come spring, merchants will fill our supply."

Her brow furrowed. "I don't understand any of this? Why don't you go to the store—*market* and buy some?" She waved her hand about. "And where are your cars? I understand how you might want to present a medieval appearance for your guests, but I haven't seen any. Are they arriving soon?" She shook out the last bits of snow from her cloak. "I have another question. Please tell me you have a bathroom...umm...loo. Yes, that's the word. I don't want to complain, but I don't relish using a chamber pot. I've mentioned this earlier to Moira and Glenna, but clearly they don't understand me. They insist that I should direct any further questions to you."

She spoke too quickly for Cormac to understand her words. Almost like his friend's wife, Brigid MacKay. How he longed for it to be spring or summer. Then he would take her to Urquhart and leave her there. Surely, the MacKays would ken what to do with the lass. Yet, the truth was, Eve Brannigan was here—in his time and the longer she stayed, the more questions she would continue to ask. And he feared only one.

He gently grabbed her elbow and steered her back toward the entrance of the castle. "Ye are wet. Go warm yourself. I will speak with Moira about providing ye with more sugar."

Eve jerked free from his grasp. "You know, Cormac, I'm tired of everyone not answering my questions. It's as if you pick the ones you understand, but ignore the others."

He started to object, but she held up her hand. "I haven't had a decent hot bath in days, and I'm tired. Don't get me wrong, I love challenging myself and have enjoyed the past few days of learning medieval life in the kitchens, but—"

"I shall have someone bring up the wooden tub to your chamber."

Her mouth gaped open in shock. "Is there running hot water with the tub?"

Cormac winced. "Nae, but ye will have hot water."

Ignoring any further outbursts from the lass, he

quickly stepped aside and made his way up to his chambers. Passing Wallace in the corridor, he instructed him to haul the wooden tub into Eve's chamber.

How long could he keep the truth from Eve? Yet, until he found a way to return the lass, no one must say a word about the year. Although, did he truly want her to leave?

Entering his chambers, he paused. "Greetings, Cathal." Removing his tunic, he placed it on a chair and strode into his inner chamber. Pulling forth a dry one from his trunk, he tugged it over his head. Striding back, he stood by the fire to warm his trews.

Cathal leaned forward in his chair. "Lively play in the snow? Or hard work?"

"A disturbance with a lass."

"Aww…Eve Brannigan."

Cormac shifted his stance. "Do ye ken the lass is *not* from this time?"

"Truly?" Cathal stroked his beard in thought.

"Dinnae claim ye did not ken. She speaks like the MacKay women for one."

The druid laughed. "Aye, she does indeed."

"Do ye have the power to send her back through the stones?"

Cathal arched a brow. "The Fae sent the lass here to this time. Clearly, they have a reason, and I wish not to alter the plans of the Fae."

Cormac pointed a finger at the druid. "What if she desires to return? Do not the Fae listen to requests?"

"Dinnae meddle with the Fae, Cormac. Ye must seek out why she was sent here."

Rubbing a hand across his face, he strolled over to

his desk. Grabbing a jug, he held it up. "Wine?"

"Please."

Filling two mugs, Cormac handed one to the druid. "Ye have yet to answer my question. Can ye send the lass back to her time?"

Cathal narrowed his lips and gazed into his mug. "It depends."

"On what?"

The druid met his stare. "If the Fae or the lass wishes it so."

"Until I can find a way to inform her of the time—"

Both men turned when shouting erupted in the corridor.

Not even bothering to knock, Eve flung the door open. "Are you serious? A wooden tub and it has to be filled with hot water? It's absurd! And here I thought you were teasing. I'm not about to ask anyone to haul buckets of water up those stairs for me."

"Ye were saying, Cormac…" The druid smiled over the rim of his mug.

Cormac gave the man a look of warning. Handing Eve his mug, he steered her out of his chambers. "'Tis the way it is done here at Creag. Until a proper bath can be made, ye will have to make do with the tub. Pray forgive me for the inconvenience."

She sniffed the contents. "Smells good. Wine?"

"Aye," he answered. "Plum."

"May I?"

Smiling, he nodded.

Cormac watched as she downed the entire contents. She blinked and then handed him the mug.

"Delicious. Now that I've warmed up, I won't

require a bath. Perhaps later, but please send your men out of my room. They have more important things to attend to. I have to return to the kitchens."

"But I have done as ye have wished. Did ye not state ye hadn't had a…what was the word ye used?" he teased.

"Decent," she replied.

Moving her along the corridor, he glanced inside her chamber. The tub set in front of a blazing fire was already half-filled. Placing his hand on the small of her back, he pushed her ahead of him. He put the mug down on the table and went to test the water.

"'Tis a pity ye would forego a fine bath. If this were in my chambers, I would strip my clothes and sink deep within."

Eve's eyes went wide. A tinge of pink scored her cheeks, and he wanted her even more.

Cormac's mind screamed at him to leave her chambers, but his feet refused to take the steps out of the room. He would give anything to see Eve Brannigan soaking naked in his tub—rubbing soap over her arms, her full breasts, dipping his fingers between her thighs.

He stalked her like a hunter, and she was his prey.

When he stood mere inches in front of her, his hand reached out and captured a stray curl at the nape of her neck. Wrapping it around his finger, he tugged. "So verra beautiful." Her lips were red, stained from the wine and with each rise and fall of her breath, he could see her own battle of lust within her eyes.

"One kiss," he murmured against her cheek. The tight knot within him begged for release.

She swallowed. "I…do…don't know."

"I will nae beg for one, Eve." He nuzzled the skin

below her ear, making him crave her even more.

"*Yes*," she whispered.

He kissed the lock of hair and desire burst forth from him. Letting the curl unravel, he grabbed Eve around the waist with one arm. Cupping her cheek, he stroked his thumb over her bottom lip. Lowering his head, his lips feasted lightly on her mouth, until she opened fully and darted her sweet tongue into him. His shy lass had become brazen. No longer gentle, he crushed her to his chest and plundered her mouth fully. He stroked her tongue, the velvet touch sending him spiraling.

She wrapped her arms around his neck, her fingers digging into his scalp and Cormac groaned. Not leaving the tempting taste of her lips, his hand moved gently up along her waist until his fingers brushed over a pert nipple. He drew her gasp into his body as he deepened the kiss. Cormac wanted nothing more than to bury himself deep within her body.

Lifting her in one swift move, he carried her to the bed and gently put her down. She was a vision lying there—her golden hair spread out against the furs. Lowering himself beside her, he wasted no time in pressing kisses along the tops of her breasts, along the side of her neck, and once more taking her mouth with savage intensity.

His hand slipped under her gown. The first touch of his fingers on her soft thigh had her breath coming out in gasps. But when his hand brushed over the silken curls, he was the one to let out a moan. Dipping one finger between her sweet folds, Cormac burned with desire to taste and feast on her body.

One hand clutched at his tunic, while the other

yanked on his trews.

"What do ye want, Eve?" His question sounded hoarse even to his own ears.

A low growl was his answer. Cormac froze. Looking over his shoulder, he saw the intruder. Fergus sat baring his teeth at him.

"Lugh's balls," he muttered. Returning his gaze to Eve, he closed his eyes. What had he been thinking? The door to her chamber was open. Anyone could have wandered by and seen them. She was his guest, not some lass to be bedded.

His body shook as he opened his eyes and moved off the bed. "Pray forgive me, Eve."

She scooted off the bed, a frown marring her lovely features. Her fingers trembled when she tried to adjust her gown.

"Here, let me help ye."

Eve smacked him away. "Don't come near me."

Wincing from her words, he nodded. "I shall leave ye to your bath."

Visibly shaken, she turned her back on him. "Good."

Snapping his fingers at Fergus, he made his way out of Eve's chamber with the dog following behind him.

Closing the door, Cormac leaned against the wall. Never in all his life had a woman have such a hold over him. Yet, Eve Brannigan ruled his heart and mind, sweeping in like the Highland mists and stealing the breath from his soul with her beauty and charm.

For the first time in Cormac's life, he cracked opened the door to his heart, and feared what would happen if he claimed Eve as his own—*forever*. Was love truly what was missing in his life? Or was it merely lust? If only his damn heart was nae involved, he would have found the answers he sought.

Shoving aside his turmoil, he strode silently down the corridor.

Chapter Ten

"The maiden made a wish under the stars on the full moon, but she forgot to sprinkle her words with love."

Eve stared at the door long after the man had left her room. Her hands continued to tremble as she clutched her gown in frustration. Cormac's touch had left her body aching in places she hadn't known existed. Tears burned her eyes, and she quickly wiped them away. Why had he apologized? Had he suddenly found her repulsive?

"He would never want a chubby girl with wild, uncontrollable hair." She yanked at her dress, hearing the fabric tear. Letting the tears fall down her cheeks, she stepped out of the material and sank into the tub. The warm water was bliss, helping to soothe away the pain of rejection.

Reaching for a cloth and a bar of soap on a small table, she scrubbed her body until it was red. Fury and hurt seethed inside of her as she dunked her head under the water. Bringing her head up, she wiped the water from her eyes. "Could any man want me?" Bringing her fingers to her lips, Eve could still taste the man. His kiss had sent an arrow of desire so powerful, she craved more.

She banished the thought. "He's not for you, Eve

Brannigan. You'll be leaving soon, so best to ignore him completely."

The words sounded hollow, and she slapped the cloth against the tub. Grabbing the soap, she did her best to lather the soap and went to work on her hair. Scrubbing her scalp until it tingled, she stood and reached for the one last bucket of clean water. Dumping the contents over her head, Eve almost shrieked. The icy water had not been heated.

"This is barbaric," she protested, as she squeezed the water from her hair. Reaching for a larger cloth, Eve stepped out of the tub and dried herself by the fire. Turning at the sound of someone knocking, she did her best to cover herself. Had Cormac returned?

"Who is it?"

"'Tis Katie," replied the small voice.

Eve's shoulders slumped. "Come in."

Katie entered, her arms full of gowns and smocks. "Sir Cormac stated ye had lost all your clothing on your way to Creag." She dumped everything on the bed, proceeding to shake out a few of the gowns. "I have been going through some of the older gowns and made them to your size. Ye are smaller, so with Nola's help, I took them in." She held out a dark blue gown with silver embroidery on the edges. "This one will suit ye well."

Eve did her best to wrap the cloth around her body and moved toward the bed. "It's too fine to be making bread in. I need something more durable."

"Och, nae, my lady. Sadly, this is all we have. Ye can wear a smock over the gown, if ye so wish. I have brought some as well."

She fingered the gown, and then sorted through the

others. There were gowns in gold, brown, green, rose, and lavender. "What are those?" Eve pointed to the flimsy looking dresses.

"Those are to sleep in, my lady."

Eve rubbed her forehead. "They're beautiful, but a pair of pajamas would have been okay with me." Tiny drops of water dotted the material, and she let out a moan. "My hair. If I don't untangle this mass, it will be a nightmare later to remove the knots."

Smiling, Katie reached for a small leather satchel. "I brought ye some combs." Handing her the blue gown, she said, "Let me help ye dress and tend to your hair." She fingered the stray curls. "'Tis a rare beauty and all here are envious."

"You can't be serious, Katie. There are times I want to chop it all off." No longer caring about modesty, Eve dropped the towel and let the girl help her dress.

"Nae," gasped Katie. "Ye should treasure your beauty. 'Tis a gift from the Gods and Goddesses. The druids say Mother Danu had a golden halo of hair around her, and when she walked, the sun touched the strands, lighting the way for all to see."

Puzzled, Eve asked, "Does everyone believe in the old ways here—beliefs? Not that I don't mind, but it seems strange."

Katie picked up one of the larger combs and motioned Eve to the chair. "Aye, if I ken your meaning. Are ye of the new religion?"

Eve shrugged. "I believe God is everywhere—be it angels, faeries, old and new. Are they not all the same?"

"We have witnessed the cruelty from both—priests

and druids. Although, here at Creag we honor the old ways. The Laird's mother believed in the one God. Sir Cormac's father built a chapel surrounded by his mother's much loved flowers."

Eve closed her eyes as Katie continued to comb out her hair. Her thoughts immediately went back toward the man. "Is Cormac an only child?"

Katie sighed. "Aye. The mistress gave birth to a girl, but sadly, she passed within days. They never had any more children."

"Hmm…how long have you been here?"

Chuckling softly, she answered, "I was born here."

Eve longed to ask more about the Murray family— how old was Cormac? What did he do when he wasn't pretending to be the great laird of Creag? Questions, which seemed utterly useless. *Simply do what you came here for and then leave with an experience to laugh over when you return home.*

"There. 'Tis a shame ye tie your tresses up on your head." Katie placed the comb on the table and went to retrieve the wet cloths.

Standing, Eve shook out her gown. "If only I had a mirror to see how I look."

"Ye do have one, Lady Eve."

"Fabulous! A modern piece of equipment," she said dryly. "And please call me Eve. We can all put on a good show for when the guests arrive."

The girl frowned in confusion. "I dinnae ken your meaning."

Eve groaned. "Never mind."

"The former mistress had one in each chamber. 'Tis in your trunk." Katie moved toward a large engraved wooden trunk and pulled out a small oval mirror.

"Good grief," muttered Eve. "Anything larger?"

Katie shrugged. "Perchance there might be one in the laird's chamber."

"You'll never find me going near his room, so no worries." Taking the mirror, Eve inspected herself. Shockingly, the face that gazed back didn't scare her. Her cheeks held a rosy glow, and curls that had escaped from her bun, framed her face. Touching her slightly swollen lips, Cormac's kisses came blazing back to torment her. She closed her eyes in an attempt to forget his taste, smell, and touch. Yet, when she opened them, Eve burned for more.

And she hated herself for being weak. *He doesn't want you!*

"Are ye unwell?" Katie touched her shoulder, jolting Eve out of her preoccupation with Cormac Murray.

Giving the girl a weak smile, Eve grabbed a smock. "I'm fine. I'm off to bake six loaves of bread. Wish me luck. I've wasted enough time on myself."

Quickly leaving the chamber, Eve made her way to the kitchens while humming a tune. When she entered, she waved in greeting to Glenna and Moira. Tying her smock on, she started to gather her ingredients. Ignoring the rest of the world, Eve immersed herself into work. These would be simple loaves. Tomorrow, she would make the specialty ones with an almond and honey paste. The women had told her the almonds were a gift to Cormac from a traveler.

Kneading the dough, she gave it a smack. *Banish the man's name.* Glenna looked her way. "My final tap of good luck before I put it into a bowl."

Glenna pursed her lips, but then went back to her own work.

The hours rolled by, and Eve wandered over to a table to await the breads. She managed to get them all in the stone oven without having to barter for room with other items baking. Sniffing the contents of a jug, she smiled. Pouring the wine into a mug, she ambled over to the corridor outside the kitchens. Leaning against the stone wall, she sipped the wine. Swirling the liquid on her tongue, she savored the taste. "Plums," she uttered softly.

"Aye. A blend made by the laird," replied Gordon, walking up alongside her.

She nodded in greeting. "I didn't know he had a vineyard here." Eve took another sip and then added, "He should consider bottling this and selling it here, or in the markets."

The man rubbed at his jaw. "I dinnae ken your meaning, but he will be pleased to hear ye have enjoyed the wine."

Eve snorted and looked away. "Your *laird* could care less what I enjoy."

"Ye are wrong."

"Don't think so," she argued and swallowed the last of the wine. "I'm the last person he wants to be around."

Gordon let out a curse.

Moving away from the wall, she glanced at Gordon. "Let's agree to disagree." Eve started to walk back inside the kitchens when Gordon grabbed her elbow.

"Hear me, Lady Eve. I am Cormac's oldest friend and guard. We grew up together. Never in all my time have I witnessed the man tongue-tied and his gut twisted over a lass. He maintains control with sweet words, drawing them forth. But nae this time. Ye have enchanted him and this he fears. His mood has become foul of late, and all have noticed. Tread carefully." Dropping his hand, he bowed. "Pray forgive me for speaking so."

Her mouth gaping open in shock, Eve stared as Gordon strolled away. "I'm confused," she sputtered.

"Sweet Mother Danu!" shouted Glenna.

Dashing back inside the kitchens, Eve slammed the cup onto the table. "What happened to my breads?"

She tapped the breads in disgust. "Did ye not take a portion from the pot?" chastised Glenna.

Eve smacked her forehead. "Blast! The leaven. I forgot!" Picking up a loaf, she turned it over. "What a waste."

"Nae," protested Moira as she peeled onions. "They can be part of the morning meal."

"Or used as a trencher for the stew," added Glenna.

Eve slumped down on the bench. "I guess I'll be baking all night." Dusting off her hands, she made to stand when Moira grasped her arm.

"Help Glenna and the others serve the evening meal. Ye can start anew in the morn."

"But I had planned on making the honeyed almond breads," argued Eve.

Moira smiled and squeezed her arm. "There is plenty of time. Now go."

Eve nodded slowly. "All right. But I'm up at dawn and will be in here all day."

"Ye can take the filled trenchers to the Great Hall," stated Glenna, as she moved from the hearth to the table, arranging trenchers filled with beef, salmon, and onions.

Managing to carry two trenchers, Eve maneuvered past Nola who was entering the kitchens. Flashing the girl a quick smile, she strolled toward the Great Hall. Her nerves skittered, knowing *he* was in there. Upon entering, she kept her focus on not stumbling, but her eyes deceived her and she looked across the room searching for Cormac. However, he was nowhere in the vast room. Some of the guards were sitting at the long side tables, chatting quietly, but for the most part, the hall was empty.

Sighing, she silently berated herself for wanting to see him. Gordon's words left her unsettled, and perhaps it was best she didn't run into the man.

"Do ye plan on standing all evening holding the food?" The burr of his voice rumbled low and seductive.

Eve shivered, afraid to turn around, her fingers digging into the trenchers. "No," she uttered softly.

Cormac moved to face her. "Then let me help ye." Reaching for one, his fingers brushed against her hand. Memories of what he had done earlier made her face burn, along with other places he had touched.

"Thank you," she mumbled, quickly stepping away and placing the other trencher on the table. Swiping at a loose curl, Eve wanted to flee the hall. However, he moved to block her path. She swallowed, overwhelmed by the magnitude of his presence.

"Would ye care to join me at my table?"

Eve met his gaze and lifted her chin. "I'm needed in the kitchens."

He boldly took her hand and placed it in the crook

of his arm. Leaning close to her ear, he whispered. "I have already spoken with Glenna and Moira."

Moving her along, she tried to pull free from his steely grasp. "I'm a mess," she hissed.

Cormac's laughter slithered down her spine—soft and warm. "I disagree." He turned to face her before the table. Taking his thumb, he swiped away the flour she knew was on her cheek. His hands slipped around her waist and undid the knot from her smock. When the garment came free, Eve let out the breath she was holding. The man was far too close. He invaded the air around her, smelling of wine, leather, and his own scent. The silver torc he wore around his neck glinted in the glow of the candles.

Without thought, Eve reached up and touched the warm metal. "Beautiful animals."

His lips parted, and his eyes darkened with desire. "For the hounds of Cuchulainn."

Her gaze never wavered. "You must tell me the story sometime. It's one I've forgotten."

He snatched her fingers and brought them to his lips. Placing a kiss along the knuckles, his smile contained a sensuous flame. "With pleasure." Leading her to a chair, he motioned for her to take her place.

The sound of children's laughter entering the hall silenced any further conversation. A few of the other guards had strolled inside, along with other women and children. Soon the hall was buzzing with many people. Gordon made his way to them and took a seat across from her.

Grizel and Nola dashed to her side, pleading to sit beside her. Cormac waved his approval, and the two shouted gleefully. Before long, Tomas appeared and took a place next to Gordon.

"Is there any apple buns?" asked Grizel, nudging Nola.

"Only a few and they are for the laird."

"Ye may have the last, Grizel," commented Cormac, handing her the basket.

"Och, *nae*, Sir."

"I have had my fill today," he responded.

Eve touched the girl's arm. "There will be plenty come Yule. I'll make more."

"Thank ye, Sir Cormac." Grizel took out a bun as if the item were a precious jewel.

Reaching for a jug of wine, he poured some into Eve's cup. "I fear the requests are many with all the fancy breads ye are making. Ye may find yourself chained to the ovens."

Shrugging, she picked up the cup. "I'll leave the recipes for Moira before I leave."

His hand froze over the rim of his cup and silence descended at the table.

"Where would ye go?" asked Nola in a shocked voice.

Eve took a sip of her wine. "I'm returning home after Hogmanay."

"The Fae are sending ye back to your time?"

"The Fae...as in faery? Umm...no. I'll travel by plane. And the only time I know is the current one of 2016. You're all so wrapped up in this pretend world you've forgotten your own date. I have to go back to my real home—my own life." Yet, for a moment, Eve thought staying wouldn't be so bad at all, especially with the handsome Highlander sitting next to her.

"2016," gasped Nola.

"Yes," countered Eve.

"Nae." The girl kept shaking her head.

Slowly, Eve placed her cup on the table and looked at the gathered group. Cormac glared at Nola, his eyes warning her not to say another word. A sense of dread washed through Eve. Even the children believed they were living in some medieval fantasy. It wasn't real— none of this.

The room was too small, too crowded. She had to get out of here. Now!

"I'm sorry, but I've lost my appetite. Pounding headache." She stood so fast, the chair wobbled.

"Eve." Cormac's tone held a warning, but she was scared.

Her steps quickened, leading her straight to the entrance. Shoving the castle doors open, the blast of cold air slapped at her face, but she ignored the icy sting. An urge to get free from this place overtook her and soon, Eve was running. They were all mad, or something was horribly wrong with her. She refused to believe the latter.

Steel bars greeted her. The gates had been closed. Her gazed traveled beyond the bars that kept her a prisoner. It was bleak, foreboding. She had to believe there was a modern civilization out there—somewhere.

She yanked on the gate. "Let me out," she shouted.

"Ye cannae leave."

"Why?" she yelled, glancing over her shoulder at Cormac. "Tell me why I can't leave and go home?"

"Truth?"

"Yes, damnit!"

"Because your home has yet to be discovered. Ye have crossed the veil of ages into the year 1207."

Chapter Eleven

"Let the light of the Solstice warm your heart and bring truth to your mind."

"You're mad," she hissed. "Let me out."

Cormac raked a hand through his hair. This was not how he foresaw telling the lass. Her eyes were wide with fear, but anger sparked within those green depths as well. "I cannae let ye out of these gates. 'Tis dark and nae place for a lass to be wandering. Furthermore," he held his hand up, "snow is falling."

Eve turned her back on him, her hands still clutching the steel bars.

"I ken 'tis hard to fathom. Come dawn, if the snows are light, I can take ye out of the castle and show ye the land. Trust me, Eve," he pleaded.

"You promise?"

When he touched her shoulder gently, she stiffened, but refused to turn around. "On my honor," he replied, and dropped his hand.

Turning around, she hugged her arms to ward off the chill of the night air. "Good, because right now, I'm thinking you're all a bunch of raving lunatics."

Smiling, Cormac held out his arm. "I ken some of your words and agree. 'Tis madness that ye could have traveled so far—into another year."

Taking his offered arm, she countered, "Insanity."

Placing his hand over her trembling fingers, he smiled. "I can assure ye, Eve, ye are nae the first lass to travel the veil of time."

"Really," she said dryly. "Is this what you tell others when they happen to get sucked into your illusions?"

"I dinnae ken your meaning."

"No matter. I'm not prepared to give you a lesson in the English language."

Did the MacKays have this much trouble with their wives who traveled the veil of ages? Aye, he did recall the sharp tongues from those women, and he smiled. They were perfect for his friends.

Eve pulled on his arm. "Have you not heard a word I said?"

He halted their stride. Cupping her chin, the mere touch sent a path of longing through his body. Her skin was soft and warm. He lowered his head near her ear. "Every word," he lied.

Her sweet lips parted, and Cormac ached to steal a kiss.

"Sir Cormac!" shouted Tomas. "'Tis gone and 'tis nae me this time."

Cormac let out a sigh and turned toward the running lad. "Pray tell what is missing?"

The lad rubbed his nose on his sleeve. "The spice box. Glenna is searching madly, and Moira is yelling."

"By the hounds," he groaned. "Has everyone gone mad?"

"Obviously," replied Eve.

Ignoring her comment, Cormac asked, "Have ye seen any of the other lads near the kitchens? Back? Front?"

Tomas shifted uneasily. "Ye would want names?"

"'Tis a grave concern, Tomas."

The lad glanced down at his feet. "May I whisper their names to ye?"

Eve knelt in front of the boy. "I'll turn around and place my fingers in my ears, so I won't hear a word."

He quickly glanced up. "Truly?"

She smiled and stood. Turning around, Cormac watched in awe as the lass placed two fingers inside her ears and started to hum a tune.

Tomas cupped a hand over his mouth to stop the laughter from bubbling forth. Cormac bit the inside of his cheek to keep from laughing himself. "Give me the names, or shall I guess?"

"Ye may guess and I will nod," replied Tomas.

"Ranald and Bran."

Tomas nodded.

"Return to the kitchens and let Moira ken I will have the men help in the search."

The lad scampered off toward the kitchens.

Cormac waited until the lad was inside before tapping Eve on the shoulders.

She bit her lower lip. "It's only a spice box, Cormac. Can't you—"

"'Tis the thirteenth century. The spice box has value." Grasping both Eve's hands, he placed a kiss across her knuckles. "I shall require your calm spirit in helping to solve this latest misfortune."

Her brow furrowed. "I'm still on the fence about the year, but I will do my best to help you."

Smiling, he took her hand and placed it in the crook of his arm. "Let me alert my men. Please tell Moira all will be well."

Eve snickered. "You're sending me into the lion's den? I think I'll need to borrow your sword to face Moira."

Stepping through the entrance, Cormac released his hold. "I trust ye can tame the fire in the woman."

"You have great faith, *Sir* Cormac," she teased as she made her way to the kitchens.

Gordon greeted him at the entrance. "'Tis true? Moira's spice box has gone missing?"

"Aye," nodded Cormac. "Have ye seen the lads, Bran and Ranald?"

"Briefly. They snatched some food and made haste out of the hall. Ye dinnae believe…Lugh's balls!" He pounded his fist into his other hand. "How dare they—"

Cormac held his hand up to stay his words. "I cannae say they were the ones to remove the box. They were seen near the kitchens. Until I have spoken with them, I await judgment."

Both men turned as Eve came running down the corridor. She grasped Cormac's arm. "Moira is calmly situated. I told her you had the entire castle searching for her spices—"

"'Tis a spice box," interrupted Cormac.

She waved him off. "Whatever. She's relieved to know you're assisting in the search. However, she has requested the pear wine from your cellar."

Cormac rubbed a hand across his face. "There is only one bottle left. The merchant from France has promised to bring more, but not until early summer."

Crossing her arms over her ample bosom, she glared at him. "You've requested I calm the woman. Now that I have, don't expect me to return *without* the bottle. If you have no plans of relinquishing the wine, *you* go and tell her."

By the hounds! What would the lass be like in his bed? Fiery? Passionate? A siren to tame? Or would she tame him with her words, her hands, her kisses on his skin? Cursing himself for where his thoughts were leading, Cormac replied, "Let me retrieve the last bottle. No doubt, the woman plans to drench a cake with the costly liquid."

"I will start searching for the lads," uttered Gordon, trying his best not to smile and failing miserably as he quickly walked away.

"Come with me," ordered Cormac.

Making his way down the long corridor, he veered right along a narrow pathway. Only one torch was lit along the wall, and he pulled it free from its holder. When they reached the door to the cellar, he handed the torch to Eve. Removing the key from his neck, he unlocked the door.

"Why do you have it locked?"

He glanced over his shoulder at her. "If I didn't, the cellar would be empty."

"Ahh…thieves everywhere." Her tone was laced with mirth.

Retrieving the torch from her hands, he moved along the walls and lit several more, placing the torch in an empty holder.

"My goodness, Cormac. Now I understand what you meant. There must be a hundred bottles down here."

"Close to a thousand," he corrected.

She stood on tiptoe trying to look at the bottles. "I'm impressed." Turning toward him, she smiled. "It's beautiful down here, too. This is your haven, right?"

His mouth twitched in humor. "Dinnae ken your meaning."

"A place to escape and rest. In my time…" Eve pointed a finger at him. "Merely saying for the moment, but in *my* time, they would call it a man cave." She trailed her fingers over the back of his chair. "How perfect. All you need is a good book and a glass of wine to shut out the noise of the others."

He leaned against the table and watched her roam the room. Never before had a lass ventured into his cellar. This was a part of his life he did not share with anyone, even his men. Yet, for some unfathomable reason, Cormac wanted to share this place and more with Eve.

She peered down the corridor. "What's in the back?"

Pushing away from the table, he strolled over to her. "Where the magic happens."

Eve pursed her lips as if considering his words. "Can you send me back home, Sir Magician?"

Cormac stepped closer, unable to stop himself. "Do ye wish to leave, Eve?"

Her lips parted, but no words came forth. She reached for his hand and turned it upward, tracing her finger down the middle of his palm. "I'm undecided." Her smile was beguiling. "I must first see if you are truly who you say you are."

He trembled from her touch. "And how can ye tell?" His voice remarkably hoarse.

"Some say the lines in your hands can tell a lot about a person. Their life, marriage, children, and who they really are." Her finger continued to trace lazy circles, and Cormac's groin tightened.

"And what do my lines tell ye?"

"You are a strong man, Cormac Murray. Bold, stubborn, loyal." She dropped his hand. "Long life."

He could still feel her burning touch within his palm. "Nae wife—children?"

"Difficult to determine." Eve swallowed, but held his gaze. "What magic do you perform down here?"

Cormac placed a hand against the wall above her shoulder, pinning her against the wall. "I make...wine."

"Oh." The word came out on a sigh.

The door to the cellar slammed, and Eve jumped right into his arms. His hands roamed down her back, and he fought the desire to take her up against the wall. "Ye feel good in my arms, *leannan*."

"Should you not check to see why the door closed?" she asked in a hushed tone.

Cormac lowered his head and brushed a kiss across her cheek, and then trailed more along her chin. "Are ye frightened?"

"Yes," she blurted out.

He lifted her chin with his finger. "Why, Eve? I will always protect ye."

"Because you make me feel things I've never felt before. You confuse me. This place baffles me, and now you're telling me I'm not in my own time."

Sighing deeply, Cormac took a step back. Her emerald eyes sparkled with desire, but this time, he held back. What could he offer her? A tumble in his bed was not for her. Nae, she deserved more. A home with a husband and children—someone from her own time. He had to put some distance between them. "Stay here."

Walking to the door, he opened it and glanced down the corridor. "No one there," he replied and closed the door. Turning around, he clasped his hands behind his back. His mind screamed at him not to speak, but his body—*nae* his heart deemed otherwise. "I will not force ye, Eve, but ken this…I want ye like no other. 'Tis an aching need and grows with each passing day. Ye speak of torment, but mine *burns*." He shifted his stance. "I will seek out the druid, Cathal and find a way to return ye to your own time. From this moment forward, I will nae bother ye."

"No," she stated firmly. "Unacceptable."

He arched a brow, stunned by her words. "Nae?"

She slowly made her way to him. When she stopped mere inches from him, her hand reached up and brushed away a lock of hair from his face. "What I mean…" She cleared her throat quickly. "I'm tired of being afraid, Cormac. Tired of fighting this desire between us. Tired of feeling I'm not worthy to be made love to." She placed a trembling hand on his chest. "Take me to your chambers," she blurted out.

Cormac's heart stopped for a second, unable to fathom Eve's words. His breath caught as he read the passion in her gaze. Hands that were fisted tightly behind him reached out and crushed her against his chest. His mouth swooped down to capture hers, drinking in the sweetness of her lips. Her tongue teased along the edges of his, and Cormac groaned, deepening the kiss. When he broke free, he cupped her face. "Are ye sure, *leannan*?"

"What does the word lea…leannan mean?" Eve whispered.

He leaned near her ear. "Sweetheart."

She licked her lips and then nibbled his chin. "Make love to me, Cormac, *please*."

Never before had he desired a woman thus. She was a gift, opening herself to him, and he ached to unwrap and take what Eve offered.

He kissed her soundly. "Wait here." Opening the door, Cormac glanced down the corridor. Muffled noises came from the Great Hall, but all else was quiet.

Motioning her outside, he quickly locked the cellar door. Cormac grabbed her hand, and made long strides toward his chambers. Hearing one of his men approach, he shoved them both into a tiny alcove. He wanted nae interruptions. Nae problems to solve. Only Eve's soft body under his own.

Feeling her shaking against his chest, he thought she might have reconsidered, until he determined she was laughing.

"By the hounds, stop," he whispered near her ear, "or I shall lift your gown and take ye against the stone wall."

Eve glanced up at him. "Standing? Really? Hmm…"

He rolled his eyes.

When the threat of someone seeing them passed, he pulled her along up the stairs. Cormac paused before his chamber. Placing his hands on her shoulders, he looked into her eyes. "Once I take ye inside these chambers, ye are mine, Eve. Do ye understand? Ye will be in my bed and no other."

"I am yours…tonight."

"*Always*," he argued. When she started to object, he covered her mouth hungrily, silencing her words.

Chapter Twelve

"In the light of the pale dawn, the truth can be seen through the prism of the Yule colors."

Flinging open the door to his chambers, Cormac led her inside and swiftly closed the door. Bolting it firmly, he turned around and Eve flung herself into his arms. She took his mouth with savage intensity igniting a firestorm within his body. Her warm, sweet, lush lips made him crave more. His tongue stroked her bottom lip as his hands roamed over her, tugging at her laces.

Cormac's fingers shook as he tried to be gentle. "Turn around," he ordered while nuzzling her neck. Pulling his *sgian dubh* out, he sliced through the bindings.

"Cormac," she gasped on a giggle.

"Shh…I will fetch ye another." Brushing a kiss to the nape of her neck, he watched Eve shiver.

His finger trailed a path on her skin down her back. "Have I found a pleasure spot?" he asked while tugging her gown free from her shoulders.

Eve glanced over her shoulder. The look she gave him pierced his soul. "Everywhere you touch gives me pleasure."

"I want to see ye naked, so I can kiss every inch of your body." He turned her around to face him. She clutched the material to her chest. Cormac removed her hands, and the gown tumbled to the floor in a soft swish. A blush stained her face and spread down her neck as she placed her hands in front of her body.

"Sweet Mother Danu...ye are beautiful, Eve."

"I don't think I am," she uttered softly.

"Have ye never been told?"

She shook her head, the curls bouncing everywhere. "No."

Cormac stepped closer, his fingers brushing away a lone curl from her breast. The rosy pert bud beckoned him to taste. "Then let me be the first. Ye are a Goddess, and dinnae let anyone tell ye otherwise." Cupping her breast, he bent and flicked his tongue over the nipple before taking it fully into his mouth.

Eve shuddered. "Oh my..."

Trailing a path of kisses to the other breast, Cormac teased and savored the taste of Eve—sweet, like honeyed cakes, and he wanted to bury himself inside her. She squirmed and gasped, digging her fingers into his scalp.

Lifting her into his arms, she placed her hands on his chest. "Not fair. Your clothes are still on," she uttered softly.

Lowering her slowly onto his bed, his eyes roamed over her body sprawled out on the furs. His smile became predatory. "So ye want to see me naked, aye?"

"Yes," she replied, partially parting her legs to reveal her hidden core.

Cormac softly swore, fearing he would spill his seed right there. She had no idea the power she held over him. A mixture of shyness and siren, drawing him to her like no other. Quickly removing his tunic, he tossed it to the floor. Unlacing his trews, his swollen cock jutted free.

"You're magnificent," she said, rising up on her knees. "May I touch you?"

Her question resembled more of a plea, and he could only nod his reply.

Scooting near the edge of the bed, she gently traced a finger down his length. Cormac let out a hiss and clenched his hands. His eyes followed her movement as her hand went lower, cupping his aching balls.

"So soft…and hard," she said softly.

When her hand returned to his cock and squeezed, stars danced before his eyes, the pleasure too much for him to bear. Grasping her hand, he pulled her back onto the furs and plundered her mouth, his hand caressing one breast, kneading and pulling on the pert nipple. He swallowed her moans, filling his lungs and wanting more. She drove him to madness.

His fingers glided over the soft curves of her flesh—down her abdomen, across the swell of her hip, until they brushed over her curls. Parting her sweet flesh, Cormac dipped a finger inside. She was hot and wet, but he would nae take her, not yet. Taking his thumb, he swept a lazy circle around her womanly center, and she arched madly against his hand.

"Cormac," she cried out, placing her hand over his.

"Does this please ye?" he growled.

She whimpered on a nod.

"Open your eyes, *leannan*."

Eve opened them slowly, and his breath hitched. "Ye have the most beautiful eyes. When ye are angry, they take on the colors of the green forest. But seeing ye spread out beneath me with desire flushed on your skin, the color reminds me of the grasses in the glen during spring."

"I never knew," she said softly.

Cormac removed his hand and placed it over hers. "Do ye like to pleasure yourself?"

He smiled when she rewarded him with a blush that extended from her face to her breasts. Cormac watched in utter fascination as she moved her fingers over her womanly center. Her gaze never wavered from his, yet, when her breathing came out in short gasps, he drew her hand away.

Lowering his head near her ear, he whispered. "Nae. Ye will come only when I am inside ye."

She reached for his strained cock, but he was faster and grabbed her hand.

"You're tormenting me, my laird."

He nipped the soft skin below her earlobe. "I have only begun, my *leannan*."

"Cormac," she whimpered, as he feasted on her breasts.

"Hmm...ye have the most delectable taste. I shall have to savor more," he teased, glancing up to see her reaction.

"Wh...what are you doing?" she gasped when his hands held her hips in place, and his tongue trailed a path down her stomach.

Eve tried to squirm away, but his hands were too strong—too powerful. She was vulnerable under his ministrations. And with each touch, each stroke of his tongue, she longed to see what he would do to her next.

She couldn't look away, mesmerized by what she longed for him to do to her body. Overwhelmed by the combinations of sensations—a brush of his fingers parted her flesh down below. But when he blew across her curls, her heart froze. Would he dare to put his mouth there? His gaze was predatory, seductive, and he held her captive.

"I have longed to taste ye here." His voice hoarse with desire.

He set his mouth to the place where she most desperately needed him, and Eve surrendered as the first flick of his tongue entered her. Her hands dug into the furs as the first wave of pleasure prickled across her skin. His mouth was glorious, his tongue driving her body to a bliss she had never encountered. Her breathing became labored, and she watched in a sensual haze everything Cormac was doing to her.

He drew back, and Eve let out a protest. "Don't stop."

"Nae. Remember, ye come when I am inside ye." Cormac prowled over her, capturing her moan with his mouth. He drew the breath from her lungs and then gave it back to her. Eve opened fully, feeling his hard length nudge her.

Ever so slowly, he guided himself inside—inch by inch. His hand slid under her bottom, and he thrust deeply into her. Crying out in exquisite bliss, Eve succumbed to his assaults, fisting her hands through his hair and urging him onward. She writhed in pleasure when his hard length stretched her further. He was a master at lovemaking, sending her trembling into an abyss—both frightening and desirable. His breath labored—the movements coming faster.

Eve raked her nails down his back. "I want…need," she sobbed out.

"Feel, *leannan*…let yourself go with me inside ye," he growled, rubbing his face against her cheek. "Ye are mine!"

She let go, surrendered, and opened herself fully—body and soul. And on a cry, Eve soared on a wave of ecstasy, flying beyond the stars. Her lips found their way instinctively to his. She kissed him, lingering, savoring his taste, and then Cormac uttered his own guttural release deep within her.

His hard body stayed atop hers for several moments before he gently rolled them over, pulling the furs over their still joined bodies. Eve could feel his racing heartbeat against her chest, mirroring her own beats.

Eve was blissfully sated. Content. Happy, being wrapped in Cormac's powerful arms. However, her mind would not shut down. He told her he wanted her *always*, not only this night. Her fear of herself made Eve doubt his words. Yet, for the first time in her life, this medieval man made her feel beautiful. *Medieval? How in the hell did she travel back in time?* She had shoved aside her earlier conversation with him, fearing he was telling the truth. A truth Eve was definitely not willing to accept. Time-travel happened in faerytales and romance stories, not in real life.

Or did they? She had often scoffed at scientists spouting nonsense, when they said time was many layers, each one unique. Had any of them managed to time-travel?

Everyone here didn't seem to mind that she was from another time. Didn't Cormac mention she wasn't the first lass to travel the veil of time? Who were the others? How was it possible? Eve should have paid more attention to those raving scientists. She rolled over, and snuggled her back against his chest.

"Ye are thinking too much, *leannan*," he murmured against her neck.

His breath was hot and sensual, and Eve shivered. "Sleep."

She smiled. "How can you tell?"

"I ken ye." He nibbled on her shoulder.

Eve tried to twist around to face him, but he held her firm, one hand already fondling her breast—his erection hard against her bottom.

"In such a short time? There's a lot you don't know about my life—my *former* life." She didn't believe her question foolish, since she could read the man just as easily—from his stubborn stance, defiant attitude, and desire for her.

"Aye. This is true. But I do ken ye, Eve Brannigan."

"Hmm…"

"Is that a pleasurable comment, or something else?" This time his hand traveled down to her bottom.

"Both," she sighed. A quiver surged through her veins with each brush of his fingers. "I have…umm…questions. *Cormac*…"

"Later ye can ask your questions," he said as he thrust into her from behind.

"*Yes…*" She could feel the rumble of his laughter.

The sensation was different, and Eve relished this new position. She couldn't remember what she wanted to say as the man moved slowly within her. He teased her with his other hand in lingering touches. His expert handling sent her to even higher levels of ecstasy.

"I cannae get enough of ye. I want to bury myself in ye and stay there forever." The burr of his voice sent a thrill of excitement down her back. When he rubbed his rough chin on her shoulder, she gasped at the exquisite pleasure.

Her body started to quake as the tremor of release built. Yet, he pulled out completely, and Eve moaned in protest. "No—"

Cormac swiftly turned her over and in one swift move, entered her fully.

They both cried out in unison. Taking her hands, he held them above her head and moved again in earnest. Eve matched his thrusts, each one more powerful than the last. The orgasm slammed into her so violently, she screamed out his name, barely hearing his own cry of release.

She floated high on the peaceful bliss, and in the silent moments that followed their lovemaking, Eve realized her life would never be the same.

Had she not vowed to never love a man? To do so, would be to open her heart to heartache, and that's exactly what had happened. Yet, her heart ignored what her mind had willed it to do for years.

And the man had slipped behind the chains protecting her heart. He'd unlocked a treasure chest of feelings—ones she vowed to never give, since she believed herself not worthy.

However, this man—*this Highlander* had stolen her heart and soul, and Eve was totally, undeniably, completely, head over heels in love with Laird Cormac Murray.

Yet, her greatest fear squashed the happiness she felt.

What if he could not love her in return? The mere thought sent a tremor of unease disturbing the happiness she'd experienced only moments before.

Chapter Thirteen

"The knight made a bracelet of faery flowers to bestow to his beloved on the Winter Solstice."

Warmth infused his spirit as Cormac slowly awakened. His body longed to take Eve again—to hold her in his arms. Never before had he experienced so much joy with another woman. She filled the emptiness within his soul. His hand glided across the furs in search of his love, but instead found his bed empty of the lass. He bolted upright and rubbed his eyes. Blinking several times, he glanced around. No trace of Eve remained except for the scent lingering in his bed.

Light streamed into his chamber, and he cursed.

Throwing off the covers, he wandered over to the table and poured water into a basin. Splashing his face with the icy water helped to remove the remnants of sleep and douse the fire burning in his body for a buxom, beautiful lass with eyes that stole his breath each time she glanced his way.

Hearing laughter, Cormac paused in his ablutions and strolled over to the window. Glancing down, he was unprepared for the sight that greeted him. In the center of the courtyard stood Eve, children surrounding her as she built some kind of beast with snow. The lass shrieked with delight, hugging one of the lads. The children seemed to enjoy what she was doing as well.

Noting one of the older lads behind her cupping a ball of snow in his hands, Cormac braced his hands on the window ledge. "Nae, ye would not dare."

To his horror, the lad threw the ball of snow at Eve's back. Fury seethed inside him. Yet, Cormac's mouth dropped open, when she turned, laughed, and then proceeded to scoop up a handful of snow and throw it back, hitting him squarely in the face.

"A good one, Eve!" shouted Cormac.

The children took turns at tossing balls of snow at her, and she did her best to make sure they were hit with one, as well.

The lass constantly surprised him.

Cormac yearned to take part in the playfulness, but other duties required his attention.

He rubbed his face vigorously. Quickly dressing, he grabbed his sword and made his way out of his chambers. The smell of sweet bread had his steps leading him to the kitchens.

"Good morn," stated Moira trying her best not to smile. "'Tis late, but I am sure Nola can find ye something to eat, so ye may break your fast. And before ye ask, the spice box has been found. Some foolish person placed it high on a shelf. But I will not name names. Furthermore, I still have need of that bottle of pear wine. I only require a splash."

Great Goddess! He had forgotten to fetch the bottle of wine last eve. "'Tis great news, indeed. I shall bring it to ye later. Is there any bread?"

This time the woman laughed fully. "Aye, but I deem Eve would nae welcome finding ye have sliced into the bread she has prepared for the Yule feast."

Stunned, Cormac replied, "The lass has been

baking?" He had made love to her once more in the early hours of the new day. When he drifted off to sleep, he had thought she did the same. Obviously, his *leannan* left his bed soon thereafter.

"Since early morn. I found her singing when I hobbled in here with Glenna. She had the look of one who had not slept, though there was a rosy glow to her face."

Cormac shrugged, glancing around for anything else to eat. "The lass likes to sing and bake."

"Aye, especially when she's happy."

Unfolding a cloth, he took a small blade and removed a chunk of cheese. "'Tis good to hear. I would want only her happiness."

"I have given her the day off, Cormac, since the next few will be hectic with preparations."

He could feel the woman's questioning gaze as he walked out of the kitchens.

"Dinnae forget to have the men gather some pine branches for the kissing boughs," she shouted.

"Aye, Moira."

Although, as Cormac ambled out into the bailey, his plans for the day took a twist. The sun was shining with no threat of more snow. A perfect day to show Eve his lands—his home. They would collect the pine branches together.

So deep in his thoughts, he had no time to dodge the ball of snow that smacked him on the head.

A hushed silence descended. He narrowed his eyes at the group gathered. Their leader stood in the center with a fist to her mouth. Clearly, Eve was doing her best not to laugh at him.

He wiped the slush from his face. Dropping his

food, Cormac bent and picked up some snow. He glanced at the older lads. "Have ye not told Eve the tale of the great snow fight many moons ago?"

"The one with ye and the MacKays—the Dragon Knights?"

Cormac nodded. "Aye, Bran."

The lad's eyes went wide. "Och, nae."

Cormac tossed the ball of snow in the air. "Ye should have before ye started this game."

Eve crossed her arms over her chest. "All right, *Laird* Murray. You have my interest. Do tell the story."

He kept tossing the wet mass, feeling its weight, and then stooped to gather more. "'Twas many, many moons ago when I was a young lad—"

"You must be ancient," she teased.

Cormac tried hard not to laugh. "Aye, some have said the same. As I was saying, when I was a young lad, I dared to challenge all the MacKay brothers."

"The Dragon Knights," she corrected. Frowning, she added, "Why are they called Dragon Knights? Is this some unique Order?"

Some of the lads snorted, and Cormac glared at them.

"A verra special Order. I shall save that story for another day. May I continue telling the tale?"

"Of course," she said, smiling.

"Now, these MacKays are mighty powerful." She started to ask a question, but Cormac stayed her words with his hand. "Ye might save your questions until after I give my account."

She bit her lip. "Sorry."

For a moment, her luscious lips distracted Cormac, recalling them on his body only hours ago. Shoving the lustful memory aside, he continued, "There were four against myself. Ye see, they were boasting of all their strength. Therefore, I challenged all of them to a *playful* battle. They all laughed and mocked me, saying it would be a slaughter. They would not dare injure their friend—*me*. But I scoffed at them until they relented. One by one, I took all four MacKays within an hour. Even with their strength and skill, I proved to be more skillful with scooping, packing, and tossing a ball of snow than the mighty Dragon Knights."

Eve moved toward him. "So what you're saying is, if we challenge you to a snowball fight, we'll lose?"

"Most certainly."

She snorted. "Sounds like these Dragon Knights are weak."

Cormac leaned near her ear and uttered softly, "These men are part Fae with powers of fire, storms, water, and land. Fierce in battle, size, and strength."

Her mouth parted in shock. "What land have I fallen through time into?"

He brushed a lock of hair from her cheek. "Scotland, *leannan*. A place filled with magic."

She held his gaze and smiled. "You must tell me more…later."

"With pleasure." Giving her a wink, he strolled away from her and the children, still tossing the ball of snow and bracing himself for what was to follow.

Within moments, a barrage of snowballs pelted his back. Tossing back his head, Cormac roared with laughter. Swiftly turning around, he stalked over to their leader.

"Is that one for me?" she asked between bouts of laughter.

"Aye."

"Then throw it!"

"Nae. Must find a special place. Perchance, on your skin."

"Absolutely not!" she shrieked.

His prey's cheeks colored more under the heat of his gaze. When she lifted her gown to flee, he lunged, and they both went tumbling—the ball of snow slapping him in the face.

Gleeful shouts emanated from the children. "Lady Eve has won," yelled one of the lasses.

Cormac burst out in laughter, along with Eve. Rolling off her, he stood and brushed off the snow. Holding out his hand, he said, "I concede this one time, *Lady* Eve."

Taking his offered hand, she stood. Reaching up with her fingers, she wiped away the bits of slush from his hair. "Perhaps a rematch?"

Giving her a wink, he said quietly, "We shall discuss terms in my chambers this evening."

"I may resort to bribery," she countered moving away from him.

Quickly grabbing her hand, he placed a kiss on her wrist. "I hear ye have the day off. Would ye care to journey with me to see my lands and collect some pine branches for the feast?"

"I would love to," she agreed softly.

"Good. Meet me in the stables in an hour."

Heading for the lists, Cormac was prepared for a tongue-lashing from some of his men for sleeping past dawn, but he gave nae care. His mood was one of happiness and naught they said would dispel the feeling.

When he entered, Gordon was leaning against a pillar. The man turned and raised a brow. The others lowered their swords, trying hard to hide their smirks.

Cormac pointed his sword at the group of men. "I shall slice the tongue out of the first who dares to speak the lateness of the hour."

"None from me," replied Gordon, smiling fully. "Ye must have had a verra good reason for staying abed."

"Aye," agreed the rest of the men.

Cormac's hands itched to take a blow to Gordon's smile and remove it from his face.

His guard moved away from the pillar. "Who would ye like to spar with first?"

"None. I have other duties to attend to. Ye may continue." He stared at the man, daring him to utter another word.

Gordon gave him a salute.

Leaving the men, Cormac quickly made his way to the stables. Upon entering, he searched for his stable master. "Tiernan, where are ye?"

The man waved a hand out of one of the stalls. "In here."

Stepping over to the stall, Cormac peered inside. Tiernan glanced his way. "Broken shoe."

"I'll tell Ross to make another," stated Cormac, leaning over the edge of the stall.

"Nae bother. The smithy was here earlier. Another horse required a shoe, as well."

"I need a horse for Eve. The lass has never ridden. Do ye deem she would fare well with Shadow?"

Tiernan chuckled, tossing bits of a broken horseshoe out of the stall. "Aye, but if the lass is fearful of the animals, one look at the old beast will surely have her running for the hills."

Rubbing his chin, Cormac glanced down the stables searching for the animal. "True. Yet, he is a calm, sturdy horse."

"Shall I prepare the animal?" asked Tiernan.

"Nae. I will tend to him and my own."

"Ye might want to have words with the lass before she sets her eyes on the beast," suggested Tiernan.

As he strolled along the stables, Cormac approached the animal's stall and plucked an apple from a basket hanging on a peg. "Greetings, Shadow."

Black beady eyes fixed intently on Cormac. Tufts of his black mane stuck out in all directions, giving him a haunted, mad appearance. Although, in truth, the black beast was one of the gentlest horses he had ever encountered. He was given the name of Shadow, because everyone feared the animal and ignored him altogether. The poor beast was constantly left out.

Taking a bite from his apple, Cormac held the piece outward. "I am giving ye a bribe, my friend. Ye are to be on your best manners for a certain lass. I must confess to a secret. She does not ken how to ride a horse. Furthermore, I happen to like this lass, and I sense ye will too."

The horse ambled slowly toward him. Taking the offered treat, he devoured it in one bite and then nudged Cormac's shoulder.

"One more and then we must make ready. We want to greet Lady Eve looking our best."

As soon as the animal finished another chunk of apple, Cormac prepared him for Eve and then saw to his own horse. When he was finished, he brought them to the front of the stables. Glancing outside, he noticed Eve approaching.

Trying to tame the wild mane on Shadow, he bent near the beast's ear. "Here she comes, my friend. Remember my words."

The horse looked at him and then to Eve as she entered the stables.

Eve pushed back the hood of her cloak. "I brought some bread and cheese, since I didn't know how long we'll be gone."

Cormac nodded. "This here is Shadow. A verra gentle animal." He continued to stroke the animal's mane, praying Eve would not fear the horse.

"Goodness, you're handsome," she remarked. "I thought to bring you sugar cubes, but since it's a valuable commodity, I brought an apple. I sliced it in half to make it easier." Holding the halves in her palm, the horse proceeded to eat from her hand. Eve giggled in delight. "It tickles."

Cormac smiled fully. By the hounds! The lass had enchanted the animal. Her laughter was music to his ears, and he deemed he would never tire of the sound.

"Ye have made a friend for life," he stated.

"Good, because I certainly don't need him to toss me onto the ground." She gave him a scratch behind his ear, and the horse leaned against her hand.

"I must admit, I have never seen the animal take to someone so quickly."

"He simply needs some love, right?"

Cormac grasped both of her hands. Their gazes locked. How he wanted to say the words that had grown within his heart, but fear kept his tongue silent. Placing a kiss along her knuckles, he said, "Let me help ye onto

Shadow." Removing her bundle of food, he placed it in a bag on his horse.

"Is there anything I need to know regarding the reins with Shadow? Does he like to be guided in any particular way?" she asked as Cormac settled her onto the animal. "I do know some maneuvers, but they're from reading about them in a book."

"Truly? These are written in a book?"

"Yep."

As Cormac mounted his own horse, he rubbed his chin. "Ye must tell me all about these books."

"You like to read?"

Cormac leaned across and cupped her chin. "Perchance, I shall bring a few into my chambers this evening when ye join me."

"That would be nice," she whispered.

His lips slowly descended to meet hers. He no longer cared who witnessed his desire for Eve. Cormac had already claimed her for his own. Drinking in the sweetness of her lips, he broke free.

"Indeed, *verra* nice."

Chapter Fourteen

"Sing a song of the past. Write a verse for the present. Make a wish for the future."

Eve lifted her head to the warm sun, reveling in the day and being near a man who fascinated her. His love for his home, land, and his people was evident in the way he spoke. He'd stop occasionally, making sure she was all right as he pointed out landmarks. They ambled along at a leisurely pace and contentment flowed through her body.

The man was correct. Scotland was a land of beauty and magic. Being on a horse out in the fresh air, one could see, hear, and smell the land far better than being in a car racing at ungodly speeds. She closed her eyes and inhaled the crisp, clean scent of pine.

"Have ye fallen asleep, *leannan*?"

The burr of his voice sent shivers down her body. Opening her eyes, she smiled. "No, only enjoying the moment. Shadow is an excellent driver, and has made me relax." She patted the animal's mane.

"I ken he favors ye, too. More so, if ye take him out for a daily ride."

"I would like to learn more, since this is the method of travel. I've become quite fond of the horse." Sighing, Eve looked away.

"What ails ye?" asked Cormac moving to her side.

She glanced sideways at the man. Worry shone in his eyes as he placed a hand over hers. His fingers were strong and warm.

"There are times when the rational side of my brain has a difficult time believing"—she waved her free hand in the air—"faery magic. Trust me, I've heard enough of the stories, but I never dreamed those my mother told me were true."

Releasing her hand, he dismounted from Fingal. Moving to her side, he wrapped his arms around her waist and drew her down against his body. His gaze swept over her features. "The Fae are real, Eve. They live beneath the land between the realms. So ye did not believe your own mother?"

Nervous laughter bubbled forth from Eve. "I did when I was a young girl, but I outgrew those foolish beliefs, especially after she and my father died. My aunt took to raising me, but I buried those stories she used to tell me."

Cormac brushed his fingers down her cheek. "Do ye think I am foolish? Am I nae real?"

His simple touch sent a spark of desire throughout her body. "You are real," she said softly.

Placing his head on her forehead, he sighed. "I ken 'tis hard to fathom ye have traveled the veil of ages, but ye are now here. I dinnae ken why the Fae have sent ye." He lifted his head and frowned. "There is a Fae well nearby. Some say this place is where ye can whisper your questions to the Fae. However, only those of pure heart will be chosen to have their question answered."

Eve stared into his blue eyes, mesmerized by his words. Her mother had once told her a similar story.

"The Well of the Faery Wishes," she uttered in a shocked tone.

"Ahh…ye have heard the tale?"

"Yes. It was a tale my mother told me a long time ago. But we must bring something as a gift."

His fingers reached for a stray curl at the nape of her neck and kissed the end. "Ye could leave a lock of your hair."

Eve placed her hands on his chest. "I would happily give you one, but I have something better for the Fae."

Cormac angled his head at her. "Ye would grant me a lock?"

I have already given you my heart, Cormac Murray. "Yes."

His lips gently brushed against hers. "I will take that boon when ye are in my chambers tonight. Now show me what ye will gift to the Fae."

As he stepped back, Eve made her way to his horse. Removing some bread, she tore off a piece. Holding it aloft, she said, "Bread, particularly honeyed, is a favorite with the Fae."

"And ye have made this with your own hands," he added.

"Exactly!" Pulling out a cloth from his satchel, she carefully wrapped the offering.

Cormac helped her back onto her horse and they rode off through a dense cluster of pine and birch trees. Birds chirped, squirrels played among the branches, and once, Eve thought she spied a stag. Onward he led them while all the time whistling a tune, and she smiled.

I'm in the thirteenth century with a Highland chieftain, traveling to a Fae holy well to make a wish.

But what do I ask for?

Eve almost laughed aloud at the absurdity, but her smile quickly faded. Did she really want to return to her own time? From the moment she saw Cormac Murray, her world split in two, as if one part of Eve was in the future, and another trapped with a man she loved in the past. She had given him not only her body, but also her heart and soul. Was it all a ruse to get her into his bed? Eve quickly dismissed the thought. Cormac was not a cruel man. Yet, how did he feel?

A tree limb smacked her on the face, its sting reminding Eve she wasn't ready to hear a rejection from the man in front of her. Perhaps she should stay away from his chambers for a while. Yet, her body—no her heart screamed also at her foolishness. And Eve was by no means blind to his attraction for her. But was it only lust?

She clenched her jaw so tight she feared it would snap. *How can I continue to live in this time when what I want may not be within my grasp?*

As Cormac maneuvered them around a fallen tree, the view opened into one of splendor. Eve gasped at the small meadow before her. Sunlight filtered down like faery dust filling the area with a beauty she had never seen. In the middle was a large stone well, partially covered in moss, snow, and flowers. Trees gathered in a circle as if they were ancient guardians watching over the well and its surroundings.

Blissful silence greeted them.

Cormac had dismounted and was already at her side. She placed her hands on his shoulders as he set her down gently. "'Tis a beauty, aye?"

Moving unsteadily, Eve winced and rubbed at her

thighs. "It's gorgeous. There's definitely magic in this place."

Kissing the top of her head, he tucked her hand in the crook of his arm. "Lean on me, *leannan*."

She nodded. Making their way to the well, she could see a rabbit pop its head out from the snow. "Someone has come to welcome us."

He chuckled softly. "Nae for long, unless ye want to give up your portion of bread to the wee animal."

"Drats!" She squeezed his arm. "I left my gift on Shadow."

"Dinnae worry. I will see ye safely to the well and then fetch it for ye. I will gather some pine branches and give ye time to make your wish."

Smiling up at the man, she replied, "Thank you, Cormac."

When they reached the well, he kissed her once again before returning to the horses. Her hand trembled as she brushed her fingers over the top of the well, the moss soft and moist. Peering inside, Eve could hear the water gently lapping against the walls of the stone and a sense of peace washed through her.

"Dear Fae, I'm so confused." She rubbed her forehead trying hard to think of her question. Suddenly, her fingers froze. Her question must not come from the mind, but from her heart.

Placing both hands over her heart, she closed her eyes and breathed deeply. When she opened them, colors danced before her, and she heard the soft whisper of bells. "Although it's only been a little over a week, I know my love for Cormac is strong and real. But..." she paused and then continued, "Can the man love me in return?"

A soft breeze caressed her cheek and Eve touched the spot with her fingers. Hearing Cormac approaching, she turned around.

"Ye glow as someone who has been touched by the Fae," he uttered quietly. Reaching for her hand, Cormac placed the bread within. "I shall wait by the horses."

Nodding, she reached up and touched his face. Her heart ached to tell him the words that filled her soul. So instead, she stood on her tiptoes and kissed him, lingering, savoring every moment. His hands grasped her arms, lifting her, and he deepened the kiss. Closing her eyes, she sank into him and his strength. The air around them smelled of wildflowers on a spring day—warm and enticing.

When they parted, his breathing was labored. He took a few steps backward, before turning to leave.

Eve's body trembled—filled with a need she couldn't understand as she watched him stride away. Glancing at the well, she realized the power of the place—one filled with only love.

Slowly turning around, she unfolded the cloth. Placing the bread on the ledge of the well, she smiled.

"Thank you for hearing me, Fae."

She didn't want to leave this place. It was safe, warm, loving. Yet, the man behind her beckoned her to return. And she yearned to be with him always. Believing the Fae would grant her wish, Eve strolled back to Cormac.

****

As they traveled back to Creag, both remained silent. Cormac had only visited the Fae well once before, yet, he had never witnessed the presence of the Fae as he did that moment in the glen with Eve. The glow on her face shimmered with joy, and the light of love sparkled in those emerald eyes he had come to love. And in the quiet stillness, Cormac feared the Fae would whisk her away to their realm.

What was her wish to the Fae? To return to her own time?

An ache settled within him, and he rubbed his chest with the heel of his palm. Is this what happens when ye love another?

Cormac's back stiffened. He had broken his own vow by falling in love with Eve. He did not want Eve to return to her own time, regardless of her wish to the Fae. *I will fight ye, Fae! Do ye hear my words?*

Fingal gave a loud snort and Cormac realized he had been pulling hard on the reins. Relaxing his hands, he glanced over his shoulder. The lass rode as if she commanded the land. Her head held high and smiling.

"Where are we heading next?"

Cormac gazed upward. "Darkness is near, so we must return to Creag. Furthermore, I deem your legs will not thank me for having ye on a horse most of the day."

Eve laughed. "Nope. Already sore, but I feel confident if I ride regularly, I'll adapt."

Hope flared inside him. Perchance, his Eve planned to stay here. Cormac pointed southward. "Beyond the stream are my orchards. Apples and plums. My father planted them for my mother. She loved the fruit."

"Did you learn to make wine from your father?"

Cormac shook his head. "Nae, my father preferred ale to wine most days. A French monk lived here at Creag for a year. He taught me everything."

Her face brightened. "I would love to see them in

bloom."

"They are stunning in spring—flowers everywhere."

"Spring seems so far away." She sighed.

Will ye wait with me? Again, he could not speak the words for her to hear. Cormac gave a nudge to Fingal and they trudged onward.

"So a monk stayed here. What did he think of your old beliefs?"

Cormac spewed out a curse.

"I'm sorry. I didn't mean to offend you. I find nothing wrong with the old ways. My mother believed in them."

Bringing his horse to halt, Cormac leaned across and cupped her cheek. "Ye did nae offend me, *leannan*. I found your question amusing." Sitting back on Fingal, he smiled reassuringly. "The monk was here to visit my mother. She believed in the new religion. Although, I must confess the man did try his best to convert everyone else." Cormac gave her a wink. "He did not succeed. Yet, he remained a true friend and vowed to say a prayer when our souls left for eternal damnation to the fiery pits of Hell."

"Wow…exactly what they would say in my time."

"Truly?"

Eve burst out laughing. "Yep."

Cormac rubbed the back of his neck. "I ken that is why my father built the chapel for my mother. Not only to please her, but to make sure he did not go to this Hell."

Brushing away a lock of hair, she said, "I would like to visit the chapel."

"We have kept the place sealed since the death of

my mother. However, I shall take ye there tomorrow."

"I would like that," Eve responded.

"There is one problem—one I have forgotten," he added as they started ambling along toward Creag.

Eve rolled her eyes. "Please, no more problems for the rest of the year." She cast him a sideways glance. "I'm afraid to ask."

"I believe the keys to the chapel were buried with my mother."

"No!" gasped Eve.

Cormac realized he would do anything for her. Battle demons. Slay any beast. Even giving her his heart. "Dinnae fear, if I have to take an axe to the chains, I will do so for ye, Eve."

Chapter Fifteen

"The lovers met under the kissing bough to pledge their troth. Yet, they forgot to seal their love with a kiss."

Cormac's stomach protested fiercely as he descended the stairs. He had eaten little on his journey with Eve—happily content to watch her munch on an apple, or nibble on bread and cheese. She chatted between bites, her hands flying about to match her liveliness. When she complained he had not eaten anything, he relented. He watched in fascination as she wedged cheese and apple slices between the two pieces of bread she tore off for him. It was the most glorious meal he had ever eaten. However, his heart almost stopped beating when she nearly cut her finger with his *sgian dubh*.

As he attempted to snatch the blade from her hand, she smacked him away, informing him she knew how to handle a knife.

He chuckled at the memory and nearly collided with the golden-haired beauty coming toward him.

"Yikes! I'm sorry, Cormac." She grabbed his arm, trying to steady the trencher with her other hand.

He lifted the item from her hand as it was about to tumble free. "My pardons. My thoughts were elsewhere." Inhaling the aroma, he asked, "Wild boar with mushrooms and onions?"

"You have guessed correctly, *Laird* Cormac."

He arched a brow. "We are feasting grandly with only a few days before the Yule?"

Eve glanced over his shoulder and behind her before stepping close, as if she was about to pass along some great secret. "They're experimenting with new mushrooms and herbs from Cathal. I heard it on good authority that a certain laird must approve the dish." She gave him a wink.

Cormac inspected the dish and then lifted his finger.

"You wouldn't dare," she protested, smacking his hand away.

Lifting the trencher high over his head, he replied, "Remember, I am the laird, aye?"

Eve fisted her hands on her hips and glared at him. "And because you *are* the leader of the clan, you must show some respect."

His gaze raked over her face and settled on her lips. "I will concede defeat, but only if ye grant me a kiss."

Her cheeks flushed as she looked around the corridor. "Here?"

"Aye." As Cormac stepped closer, Eve moved backward.

"What if…someone sees us?"

Cormac's smiled turned predatory. "All I asked for was a kiss, nae to plunder your body."

When her back hit the wall, she parted her lips. "One kiss only?"

He arched a brow, understanding her meaning. "I beg for only one. Yet, later, I shall demand many more."

"Then take your kiss, my laird," she whispered.

Slowly, Cormac lowered his mouth to hers, and a moan of pleasure slipped through her lips. Powerful, hungry desire spiraled through him as her tongue invaded him, seeking, stroking. He growled, taking all she had to offer. When one of her hands wrapped around his neck, he deepened the kiss. He was lost in her touch, her lips, and Cormac burned for more.

Finally breaking free, Cormac found he was the one trembling.

"Is your arm getting tired?" she asked, breathing heavily as her hand slipped across his shoulder.

"Nae."

She gave him a gentle push back and stepped away from his embrace. "Good. I'll relieve you of the trencher, though I'll make sure to place it near you."

Obliging, Cormac handed her the trencher of food. As he strolled away, he said, "Ye may inform Moira and the others I approve of the meat."

Eve glanced over her shoulder at him. "Now why would I lie? You haven't tasted the food?"

"Och, but I have, fair Eve. From your lips."

"You're incorrigible."

Cormac roared with laughter. "I shall leave it to ye to help me make amends for my bad habits, Lady Eve."

She snorted and walked into the Great Hall.

"By the hounds…what have ye done to me, sweet lass?"

****

Cormac's eyes never veered far from Eve. Each time she arrived with some food or drink, he followed her movements. It took all his control not to order her to stay and let another help, so he did his best to remain patient. He wanted Eve all to himself, and he found his patience ebbing away. A quality that did not bode well with him.

And the evening turned late and sour.

Soon, she approached the table asking if he had enjoyed his meal. Cursing, he grasped her hand in front of his men and drew her to a nearby chair. He had expected an outburst, but she only narrowed her eyes at him before taking her place beside him.

Of course, she chatted agreeably with Gordon and Wallace, asking questions about their duties here, and ignoring him completely. Moreover, he did his best to be civil, but when Gordon leaned close and whispered something into her ear, Cormac rose abruptly, spilling wine everywhere, including on Eve.

Her gasp could be heard throughout the Great Hall. And he was the fool.

She quickly made her apologies to the men, but dismissed him with a look that would frighten even the most hardened warrior.

Cormac waited until she left and then retreated to his chambers.

Leaning against the arched window, he gazed out at the night sky. He cast a glance at his cold bed, cursing his inner demons.

He never lost control. Ever. Control was a skill he honed many years ago. His good friend, Dragon Knight, Angus MacKay, had helped him temper the anger. They were both the eldest sons—strong, leaders, and managing restraint was important for them to lead their clans.

"Sweet Mother Danu, how I miss ye, my friend. Did ye have this much trouble with the lass, Deirdre?

Aye, I believe ye did, but how did ye survive?"

He rubbed a hand over his eyes and wandered over to the furs by the fire. Cormac knew sleep would not come in his own bed without Eve in his arms. Even his dog, Fergus had left him, no doubt for her chambers.

As he stretched out along the furs, he tucked his hands under his head. "'Tis why I didn't want to give my heart to a lass. They only twist it within and spit it back out."

Grumbling a curse, he rolled onto his side and closed his eyes.

No sooner did he start to drift off than he heard someone approach from behind him. As always, Cormac kept a dirk within the furs, so he waited. As the soft whispers of feet came closer, he smiled and relaxed his body.

He did not have to turn around to ken it was Eve. Her smell invaded the chamber. She knelt behind, her fingers brushing across his shoulder.

"Cormac?" she uttered softly.

Turning over, he frowned, seeing sadness within her eyes. Cormac abruptly sat up. "What is wrong, *leannan*? Are ye hurt? Did someone hurt ye?"

Eve shook her head. "Could you explain what happened this evening? Because I can't sleep and I keep thinking I've done something wrong." She twisted the ribbons on her gown. "I was furious with you. Never before have I wanted to scream at another. Well, there was the time with these two women at my work…" She tucked her legs under her and then added, "It seems a thousand years ago. I don't like playing the part of a bitch, but I came close to stabbing your eyes out."

He groaned. "I am the fool, Eve. Ye did naught wrong. 'Twas all my doing." Raking a hand through his hair, he looked into the flames. "Ye kept coming and going, when all I wanted was to have ye near me. Aye, selfish reasons. And then I went mad seeing ye with my men."

She angled her head at him. "Do you want to know what Gordon whispered to me?"

"Aye," he replied brusquely, glancing back at her.

Smiling, she replied, "He told me to watch your reaction as he whispered near my ear."

His hands clenched the furs. "I shall hang the bastard by his balls."

"Good grief! You're wicked," she said laughingly.

"He deserves a slow punishment." Yet, Cormac could not help but smile along with Eve.

As silence settled between them, he wanted desperately to reach out and gather her into his arms. "I am...sorry, Eve."

The lass scooted toward him and placed both hands on his bent knees. Gazing into her eyes, he remained unmoving. Her touch scorched a path to his weary soul. "All is forgiven. But please don't humiliate me again."

"I dinnae ken—"

"Shh...I'll tell you the meaning of the word later. You still owe me some kisses, my laird."

Cormac wrapped his arms around her and drew her down to the furs. Leaning on his elbow, he trailed a path with his fingers over the flimsy material until he found her warm breast. "It may take all night, my *leannan*," he uttered softly, watching as her eyes took on a sensual haze.

"Ahh..." she moaned in pleasure. "Then you

shouldn't waste any more time talking, should you?" She rose to meet him in a moment of uncontrolled passion and drew his head down to meet her lips.

Her boldness undid him, stripping bare the man for only her. Eve roused not only the lustful beast, but also another part of himself. Love. The two, a powerful combination.

With each touch...each kiss...his heart swelled. Yielding to her needs, Cormac's hands explored, skimmed, teased, and delighted Eve. He had never known another to fascinate him thusly. As he roused her passion, his own grew stronger.

Stripping her free from her gown, her skin glowed by the light of the fire as his eyes roamed over her. "Your beauty takes my breath away, my love." His hand caressed the skin of her thigh, inching closer to her soft curls. Cormac dipped one finger inside her. She throbbed beneath his touch, writhing against him.

"Kiss me, Cormac," she growled.

His lips continued to explore her soft ivory flesh, finding new places of desire. Cormac fought the mounting wave of his own release, until her hand swept down over his swollen cock.

Eve nibbled along his neck, driving him mad. "Remove your clothing," she ordered.

Cormac struggled not to shatter as she continued to stroke him. His lips brushed against hers as he spoke, "I thought ye wished for more kisses?"

Reclaiming her mouth, he silenced any further words from her. His tongue sought, demanded, and she gave completely to the passion of the kiss. The coiled tension built within him, and he could nae longer hold back.

Breaking free, he moved away from her, eliciting another protest from those sweet lips. Quickly removing his trews, he knelt over her, nudging her thighs open with his hands. "I cannae hold back," he rasped.

"Then don't."

Cormac thrust deeply into her, his cry echoing her own. Fierce and passionate, their lovemaking became an urgent need to please the other. When he took her breast into his mouth, she succumbed to the abyss of pleasure, screaming his name. He loved her with reckless abandon, opening all he had within his body. When he shattered completely, Cormac's heart lurched—his release so powerful.

It was a long while before either could speak or move. Gently moving off her soft body, he brought Eve against his chest. Stroking his fingers down her back, Cormac stiffened. Lifting her chin with his finger, he gazed into eyes filled with tears. *Had he hurt the lass?*

"Why do ye weep, *leannan*?"

She sniffed, trying to wipe away the tears trailing down her cheeks. "I have never known such happiness."

"Because I give ye pleasure? Ye are beautiful, Eve."

Her brow furrowed slightly. "Is this all it is for you, Cormac? Our lovemaking is nothing more?"

"Nae," he said gruffly. *Ye have no idea how much I love ye, Eve.* The words lodged in his throat, so he said, "Ye give me pleasure, too…and I like ye verra much."

Eve lowered her head onto his chest. "Hmm…like is a good thing, I guess."

Cormac twisted one of her curls around his finger.

"I did state *verra*, *leannan*." He swallowed. "Do ye like me?"

A smile started to form around the edges of her mouth. "Like is such a vague word. No, Cormac, I don't like you…"

He froze, stunned by her words.

Eve sat and cupped his face with her hands. "I *love* you."

Shocked into silence, Cormac gathered her back into his arms, and kissed her soundly.

Chapter Sixteen

Winter Solstice—Yule 1207

"Light all the candles, so love can guide those who are lost on their path to true happiness."

Twirling a spoon by the fire, Eve fixed her gaze on the oven. She was lost in emotions and prayed the breads would rise well. Sleep never came in the arms of Laird Cormac. The man had made sure he fulfilled his quest of bestowing her with kisses over most of her skin—places that still hummed with pleasure.

When she'd woke in his bed the next morning, the man was gone. He had left with a few of his guards and went hunting. She didn't fume. In fact, Eve was relieved. It gave her time to focus on the baking and helping the others in the kitchen that day. Busy hands kept her mind from replaying the events from their time together. And when the night meal came and still no Cormac and his men, she tried in vain to push aside her doubts.

However, her mind kept playing the scene of when she blurted out her love for the man. Eve realized it was a risk, but her heart was full with happiness and contentment, and she longed to share her feelings with Cormac.

"And blast the man for not saying anything. Must

have shocked him into stunned silence," she muttered, smacking the spoon on her palm. "Ouch!"

"Whatever are ye doing, Lady Eve?" asked Ina, hobbling into the kitchens.

Eve pointed the spoon at the girl. "*Please*, call me Eve. I was lost in my own silly thoughts. And you're being foolish by attempting to walk so fast. Here, let me help you sit down."

Ina smacked her hand away playfully. "I am doing much better. John…" The girl blushed. "*Sir* John would like to dance with me at the feast, so I must make an effort to be able to walk."

"How can the man expect you to dance when you can barely walk?"

The girl's eyes went wide. "Then if I am nae there, he might find another."

Eve was so tempted to tell the girl the man wasn't worth it if she was afraid he had a roaming eye. "Gotcha. Is there anything I can do?"

Ina smiled. "Ye could help me put together the last few kissing boughs for the entry. John will be here soon to help me hang them."

Eve laughed. "You are quite the schemer."

She frowned in concentration. "I beg—"

"My apologies." Eve tapped a finger to her mouth. "Hmm…you're making a plan to trap the man under the kissing bough, so he can give you a kiss?"

"Ahh…" The girl nodded and smiled.

Following Ina to the table, Eve picked up a round ball of twigs and evergreens and watched as Ina stuck apples, rosemary branches, and cinnamon sticks into the bough. Digging through another basket, the girl pulled out some ribbons to weave through it all.

Ina's eyes sparkled with delight. "My own special ribbon."

Eve hugged the girl. "For extra providence." When she pulled back, she added, "Though, I believe he has bestowed you with kisses already, right?"

"I like him," she whispered.

Like? Eve wanted to scream at the girl. She was coming close to despising the word. Did everyone in the thirteenth century forget about the most important word of all? *Love*? Keeping silent, she bent to the task of making several more boughs.

Ina glanced over her shoulder. "John approaches."

When the guard entered, Eve realized how much he cared for the girl. His face softened. He never even bothered to glance her way as he made his way to Ina's side.

Ina stood slowly and took his offered arm.

"Lady Eve," he finally acknowledged.

Eve nodded. "Sir John." She handed him the basket of kissing boughs and watched the lovers depart from the kitchens.

Brushing her hands off, she grabbed her spoon and went to stand in front of the ovens again.

"Ye are needed in your chambers," stated Glenna as she entered the kitchens with baskets of fresh herbs.

Relieving the woman of one of the baskets, she replied, "Why?"

The woman grabbed her wrist and removed the spoon from her hand. "Ye are done in here. I can remove the breads. Go take yourself to your chambers. Katie is waiting for ye."

Eve narrowed her eyes at Glenna. "There's more work for me in here."

Glenna fisted her hands on her hips. "The venison is cooking, along with the lamb and wild boar. Onions are chopped, along with the cabbage. Mushrooms have been cleaned. The feathers have been removed from the quail—fat, spices, and bread are being mixed in the other kitchen to stuff the birds. One of the lads is tending to the salmon. Moira finished the pear sauce for your buns, and the vegetables have all been scrubbed. Furthermore, ye are taking up my time by standing here."

"Good grief, Glenna. I was only trying to help."

The woman smirked and smacked Eve playfully on her bottom. "I shall only tell ye once, but we have been blessed to have ye in these kitchens. Now leave."

Eve's mouth gaped open. "Why…thank you," she said and hugged the woman.

Quickly leaving the kitchens, Eve dashed up the stairs. Opening the door, she paused at the entrance. The wooden tub was set near a blazing fire, filled with steaming hot water. Katie stood in front of her bed with a smile that spoke of secrets.

Closing the door, Eve made her way to the girl. "What are you hiding?"

Katie stepped aside to reveal a stunning emerald gown, trimmed with silver brocade along the edges of the sleeves and neckline. Eve fingered the soft velvet material. "It's too beautiful." She glanced up at Katie. "No undergarments? Shifts?"

"Nae," answered the girl, grinning and moved to a table by the tub. "I have a fresh soap made with roses from the summer. And combs to wear, if ye so wish."

"Why all the fuss?" asked Eve, picking up the soap and inhaling the scent.

"'Tis Yule."

"But what about you—the others?"

Katie pointed a finger at her. "I have already taken my bath days ago. The laird ordered everyone that ye were to be banished from the kitchens after the noon meal, so ye could prepare for the feast."

Eve arched a brow. "Did he?" Glancing away, her heart swelled to think Cormac had a hand in all of this. "Can you help me?"

"Och, aye."

As Katie helped her out of her clothing, Eve sank her body into the heavenly water. Uttering a contented sigh, she plunged her head under. Heavenly warmth filled her body as she surfaced. "I will never take a bath for granted again. Give me a hot bath each evening, and I'm a happy woman," she muttered. Seeing Katie wince in horror, she laughed. "What?"

"Ye could risk fever."

Eve bit her cheek to keep from laughing at the silly comment. They all believed Eve crazy with her requests for bathing, even if most days it was hot water in a basin and a bar of soap.

After her body was scrubbed, Eve leaned forward. Katie worked on lathering her hair, and Eve's spirits soared. So wrapped up in Cormac and the feast, she didn't consider this was a beautiful season of joy and light. Her favorite time of year.

"Close your eyes," ordered Katie.

Complying, Eve waited as the girl poured warm water over her head with several pitchers.

Katie ran her fingers over her long locks. "'Tis clean."

Opening her eyes, Eve wiped away the water.

"Thanks." Eager to see Cormac, she stood abruptly, splashing water everywhere.

Katie burst out laughing. "I can see the bath agrees with ye, Eve."

"Definitely." Stepping out of the tub, she took the offered cloth and dried off. Katie helped her into a long smock, and then led her to a chair by the fire and proceeded to dry her hair. "You do understand my hair takes forever to dry?"

"Have nae fear, Eve. There is time."

Settling back into Katie's care, Eve closed her eyes and smiled.

****

When Cormac entered the Great Hall, he scanned the area, seeking only one—Eve. He tried not to think of her while on his hunt, but she traveled with him the entire time. Before he left, he gave orders to all and then went to his locked trunk and retrieved the one item he would present to her on this night. An emerald suspended on a silver chain. The heirloom had been passed down to each woman within the Murray clan for centuries.

Tonight, Cormac would bestow the stone on Eve.

Straightening his tunic, he made his way to the table by the hearth. Nodding to Wallace and Gordon, he reached for a pitcher of wine and poured some into a mug. He took a sip, savoring the special wine he had prepared for the feast. Glancing around the room, he noticed the tables were filled with trenchers of meats, fowl, fish, breads, and many other tempting dishes. Greenery adorned the tables, and he spied several kissing boughs tucked above the alcoves. Inhaling deeply, he smiled, pleased with everything.

Families started to make their way inside the Great Hall. Children scampered around, snatching nuts from the tables in glee. Many of the lads and lasses had lost fathers and mothers during the battles of the past few years, and Cormac made sure that Creag would always be their home. He became their guardian and protector.

"Have ye heard the news?" asked Gordon as he refilled his own mug.

"Do tell."

"John has asked Ina to be his wife."

Cormac laughed. "'Tis nae great news. The man has been smitten with the lass for many moons. I am happy for them."

"Aye. A good time for happy unions."

He glanced over the rim of his mug at his friend. "True."

"Great Goddess," muttered Gordon. His friend clamped a hand on his shoulder. "If ye dinnae claim her tonight, I will fight ye for her."

Cormac's jaw clenched when the man turned him around slowly. Stunned by the vision at the entrance of the hall, he was unable to move. Her golden hair curled around her body to her waist, shimmering from the light of the many candles that lit the hall. However, it was the gown that had him captivated. It flowed around her, hugging places he had trailed his tongue over. She glided into the hall, grasping the hands of several children. As she continued to make her way inside, several stopped to speak with her, pressing a kiss to her cheek. In return, she hugged them and smiled.

By the hounds! Did they ken what he had already? What he had never dreamed could be possible? All because a mere lass stepped into his path with sunlight shimmering off her skin. She had enchanted him instantly. Now, Eve had charmed his own people as well.

"Go greet her," suggested Gordon, removing the mug from his hand.

Swallowing, he nodded and made his way to the woman who had stolen his heart.

Standing before her, Cormac clasped his trembling hands behind his back. "Eve."

She turned toward him. Smiling broadly, she nodded. "Cormac. I take it your hunt was successful?"

"Aye." Holding out his arm, he waited.

When she placed her hand in the crook of his arm, Cormac sighed in contentment. *My woman.*

Bringing her to his table, he had no plans on releasing his hold on her warmth. Yet, another child came running to greet her, and her fingers slipped free.

Eve bent and took the gift of flowers from the lass. "They are beautiful. What are they?"

The lass giggled. "They are faery flowers."

"Heather," corrected Cormac softly.

Giving the girl a hug, she said, "We must find a small glass of water to put them into, so they won't wilt."

The young girl nodded in amusement.

His heart sank as Eve moved away, until she paused and rushed back to his side. "If I forget to mention this later, I want to thank you for the hot bath." She stood back and raked her gaze over him, adding, "You are magnificent, my laird. Royal blue is perfect for you."

Words failed Cormac as he watched her drift away.

Reaching for his mug, he drained it completely and

headed after Eve. Never again, did Cormac wish to be parted after this night.

As his steps quickened, he grabbed Eve's hand. "I believe I have found a cup for the flowers. Ye can keep them at the table during the feast."

Laughing, Eve took the mug. "All we need is water."

Again, Cormac took her hand. "I have requested a pitcher to be near ye. I ken how ye like to have your water."

She squeezed his hand. "You've thought of everything, Cormac."

All but one, which he needed to tell her now, before someone else came to greet his fair Eve. However, when he opened his mouth, the minstrels decided to start playing. How could he speak the words with so much noise?

"How perfect!" she exclaimed in delight.

The hall erupted into jubilation. One of the young lads came forth and bowed before Eve, though his eyes stayed on Cormac. "Would ye like to dance, Lady Eve?"

She turned to Cormac. "It is up to the laird."

How could he possibly deny the lad? Nodding his consent, Cormac took the flowers from Eve. Making his way back to the table, he paused to make his greetings to others. He asked if the food was to their liking and told them how pleased he was to see all was well with them.

Settling back at his table, he poured more wine into his mug and waited.

Although, as the evening progressed, Cormac's mood worsened, even after the lighting of the Yule log by Cathal. Eve became the center of everyone's attention, leaving him no time to utter what was in his heart. When she did return to his side, she barely had time for a bite of food or drink, before someone approached. The lads would beg for a dance, and the women inquired about the secret herb she used in her breads.

And as the hour grew late, the stone Cormac wanted to present to her grew heavy in his pouch on his belt.

Rushing back to his side, her cheeks flushed from the last dance, she gulped down some water. "How utterly magical this has been, Cormac."

He swirled his wine. "I am pleased ye are *enjoying* yourself." His tone sounded gruff, and he chided himself silently.

She placed a hand on his arm. "Are you angry?"

"Nae," he scoffed, pouring more wine into his mug. "Go. Enjoy another dance with the men."

Eve blanched. "Excuse me? I haven't danced with *any* of the men."

"Aye, ye did, with Bran," he corrected.

"He's only a young teen—a boy," she hissed.

Cormac glared at her. "A man in my world, Eve."

Eve shook his arm. "What do you want from me, Cormac? Tell me now. This instant."

He snorted. "Or what? Ye leave?" Downing the last of the wine, he refilled his mug.

"What a fool you are, Cormac Murray."

Standing, she leaned near his ear. "If I was sent here, I'm sure I can return. Will that make you happy?"

Her words stunned him, and he watched in silence as she left the hall. Music and merriment flowed around him, but as Eve vanished from his view, his world completely shattered. Darkness entered him, snatching away the joy within. The happiness she brought to him. His heart pounded so loudly, he felt it would burst from his chest.

Eve leave? Go back to her own time?

"Nae," he roared, standing abruptly. Shoving past the others and their questioning glances, he ran after the one who had brought light into his soul.

Leaving the Great Hall, the blast of cold air greeted him. The doors of the castle had been flung wide open. His steps hastened, but Cathal emerged and blocked his path.

"Where did she flee?" he blurted out.

"Down the path near the chapel. There is verra little time, Cormac."

Fear slithered down his spine. "What do ye mean?"

"All she need do is ask, and the Fae will return her to her own century. The doors between the realms are open this night."

He grasped the druid's arm. "I will nae lose her! This is her home!"

Cathal poked him on the chest. "Then speak your heart, for time is fleeing."

Shouting her name, Cormac ran off down the path leading to his mother's chapel. Jumping over boulders and ducking under tree branches, he kept shouting her name. The mists thickened, and his throat became thick with worry.

As he approached the chapel, the mists cleared, and starlight and the glow of the full moon cast the area in a brilliance he had never witnessed. Standing near the gnarled ancient oak, stood Eve. Yet, the shimmering light that lingered nearby had Cormac shuddering with fear. His breathing labored as he cautiously stepped forward.

"Eve. Dinnae leave me," he pleaded.

She twirled around, tears streaming down her face. "Why? Tell me now, or I'll walk through those gates by the oak and leave forever."

Emotions overcame Cormac, and he found he could nae speak.

Love not fury shone in her eyes, and she took a hesitant step toward him. "Sadly, we don't have all night. The Fae have heard my request."

"Ye want to leave?" he demanded, his heart breaking.

"Why should I stay?" she sobbed, taking another step.

"I...I want to wake in the morn with ye in my arms, and to whisper my love for ye before ye drift off to sleep."

She stood before him now. "But *why*?"

His voice shook with emotions. "Because I *love* ye, Eve." He pounded his chest with his fist. "A love that burns and consumes me each day, and I cannae imagine a life without ye!"

Cupping his face with her warm hands, she whispered, "And I love *you* with all my heart and soul."

Cormac lifted her into his arms and kissed her hungrily. Breaking free, he twirled her around in delight. "Eve, I love ye! I love ye, my *leannan*!"

She giggled and buried her face in his neck.

Lights sparkled and danced around them. As Cormac gently brought her down to the ground, they both glanced at the fading lights by the ancient oak.

Wrapping an arm around her shoulder, he held her close. His eyes misted with unshed tears as he spoke. "Ye would have walked through…left me?"

Eve lifted her head and placed her hand on his heart. "Almost," she murmured. "But I waited, praying you would follow. *If…*" She swallowed. "If I had left, I think I would have died a slow death."

Cormac crushed her to his chest. "And my heart would have been cleaved in two. Och, Eve…" Wiping away her tears with his thumb, he sought out her lips once again. "Never leave me, *ever*, *leannan*," he whispered against her cheek.

Taking her hand, he led her away from the oak tree. Letting the moonlight guide his steps, he brought her to the chapel. Cupping her chin, he gazed into her eyes. "I wanted to bring ye here after I had spoken what was in my heart. Sadly, the night did not go as I had planned."

Eve sniffed and smiled. "No, but it's ending beautifully."

"I have something to bestow upon ye." Pulling out the emerald from his pouch, he placed it over Eve's head. "This has been in our family for many generations. 'Tis meant for each Mistress of Creag."

She lifted the emerald to the glowing light of the moon and then back to meet his gaze. "It's stunning—gorgeous!"

Grasping her hands, he brought them to his chest. "Will ye marry me, Eve? Be my wife? Can ye live without things from your future? For if ye say nae, I am a lost man."

"Cormac, my home is here—a place which fills my soul. So, yes, I will happily be your wife." She traced a finger along his torc before adding, "But be warned, I'm a *lass* from the future, and I will stand by your side, not behind."

Chuckling softly, he drew her into his arms. "I would expect naught else."

Eve glanced over her shoulder. "The chapel is lovely, reminding me of a cottage. Why is it so small?"

Sighing, Cormac turned her around and wrapped his hands around her waist. He gazed at the place as if seeing it for the first time. Ivy trailed up along either side of the entrance, and he knew that in summer the roses his mother had planted many moons ago would fill the area with beauty. "It was built for only her to reside and pray. Her request was simple, and my father granted her this place. She retreated here daily—once in the morn and in the evening."

Eve gasped. "The chains are gone." She looked up at Cormac. "You found the keys?"

"Nae." His eyes roamed over her features. "I would slay anything or anyone to make ye happy. I removed the chains with an axe early this morn."

She turned around and hugged him fiercely. "You've already given me the greatest gift of all...your love."

"And ye shall *always* have my love." Cormac's lips descended over hers, sealing his vow with a soul-searing kiss.

Epilogue

Day after Yule—1207

"Are you sure he's at the chapel?" asked Eve, fidgeting with her flowers while she glanced out the window of her chamber.

"Ina saw him leave with Gordon and Wallace," shouted Katie from the corridor.

Her nerves tingled with excitement. Neither wished to wait another moment to be married. Therefore, when they returned to the castle, Cormac drew her into the Great Hall and proclaimed his love for Eve in front of everyone. He then announced the marriage would take place in the afternoon, since it was already the wee hours of a new day.

The hall erupted into gleeful shouts. Ignoring Cormac's protests, the women instantly whisked her away to another chamber. For as long as she lived, Eve would never forget the hurt look on his face. She, too, wanted desperately to be in his arms. However, they silenced her complaints with critical looks, and then told her that it wouldn't be right to spend her wedding eve in the laird's chambers.

When a dress was chosen, they left. Yet, sleep never came to Eve. And when the first light danced across the floor of her chamber, Eve bounded out of bed. Never again would she spend the night alone without her Highlander.

"'Tis time," announced Katie, dashing inside. She clasped her hands to her chest. "Ye are a vision in the white gown, my Lady."

"No, Katie. Only Eve. And please don't start to cry again, or I will, too."

The girl laughed. "I ken all will shed tears, so nae matter when we do so."

Eve nodded. "Let's go greet the laird." Reaching for the cloak she received from the gypsy woman, Ailsa, she smiled. *I truly believe in the Fae now, Mom.*

Katie helped her with the cloak and fastened it with a silver brooch. Another gift from Cormac, which arrived at her door early in the morning from his guard, Gordon.

As they made their way out of the castle, Eve fingered the emerald around her neck. With each step, her heart beat faster. Lifting her face, she let the warm sunlight fill her body. *My wedding day. Our wedding day, my love.*

Eve could see everyone—some standing along the path, tossing out flowers as she passed them. When she walked by the giant oak, Eve bowed in reverence. Craning her head, she saw him—*only* Cormac. The others all faded from her view as she made her way to the man she loved. His ivory tunic was belted with leather, and Eve could make out the dragon in the center. His hair gleamed in the sunlight and she had to blink. *You must have been chiseled from a Celtic God.*

He instantly stepped forward and grasped her hand. "'Twas torture not seeing ye all these hours," he murmured against her cheek.

She smiled. "I didn't sleep either."

Cormac winked. "And ye shall find nae sleep tonight."

Goosebumps traveled over her skin in anticipation. "Can we skip the feasting?"

His eyes flashed with desire. "Ye will be my feast." Placing her hand in the crook of his arm, he brought her to stand in front of the chapel. The doors were open, and Cathal stood to the side.

The druid waved his hand to the entrance. "I have heard those who pledge their vows in the new religion do so in front of the doors."

Eve looked to Cormac. "I wish to say our vows here in the sunlight surrounded by everyone." She turned to Cathal. "I know Cormac wishes it, but I also would be honored if you would give us your blessing." Cormac squeezed her hand.

"Ye have *honored* me, Lady Eve," stated Cathal and moved to their side.

Closing his eyes, he lifted his arms upward. "We are gathered here in this sacred place—a blend of old and new to witness the joining of Cormac Blaine Murray and Eve Catherine Brannigan. Two souls brought together by the Fae with the blessing of Mother Danu." The druid withdrew a crimson cord from his robe. "If I may, Lady Eve?"

"Of course."

As Cormac lifted their joined hands, Cathal wove the cord around their wrists. "Ye may state your vows."

Cormac smiled and placed their joined hands on his chest. "From the moment ye stepped into my path, the world, *my world* stopped. That verra day, ye entered within me. Ye brought warmth where there was none. My heart is your home. When ye are weak, I will be your strength. Your sorrows shall be mine, and your joys will fill my soul. And when I take my last breath, your name shall be on my lips."

Tears threatened to spill forth, but Eve could not hold back the joy she felt in her heart. "I had forsaken love until the moment I glanced up and there you were. Never have I laughed, cried, or loved as much since I met you. When dark clouds threaten to spill around you, I will be there to bring the sunlight—to banish the shadows from your heart. Always and forever will be my vow—from this life to the next. The love I have given freely will never be taken away. It is yours even when I walk through to the other realm—be it Fae or Heaven."

Cormac placed his forehead on hers. "I love ye like no other, Eve. Ye steal the breath from me each time I am near ye."

"I never realized love could be so powerful," she said, her lips brushing against his.

As they both broke free, Cathal placed a hand over each of their heads. "Let the binding vows be sealed forever, and may we ask the Fae to shed their light and love along your journey in this life."

Removing the crimson cord, the druid stepped back. "Blessings to Laird Cormac Murray and Lady Eve!"

Drawing Eve to him, Cormac's mouth covered hers with a passion that sent her senses spinning.

A joyous roar erupted forth from all gathered.

When he broke free, Eve whispered, "I shall demand more of those kisses later."

His laughter sent a shiver of excitement through her. Leaning near, he said, "After the first round of best

163

wishes, I am taking ye to *our* chambers."

"And let the others celebrate without us? I'm shocked," she teased. Giving her husband a wink, she turned and embraced the children rushing toward her.

****

Cormac held his naked wife on his lap, brushing his fingers down her back in lazy circles. The fire had burned low, but he had no wish to leave the comfort of his beloved.

He had kept his promise to Eve. As soon as Gordon raised his cup at the feast stating his best wishes, Cormac lifted his wife into his arms and proceeded to carry her out of the Great Hall. Shouting and laughter surrounded them, but he gave no care. Eve was now his wife. Forever.

For the first time in his life, Cormac understood his father. And in a silent prayer, not only thanked him, but also asked for his forgiveness and his blessing.

"Would you like more?" asked Eve as she held out a piece of honeyed bread with pear sauce.

"Mmm…I have never tasted finer. I must purchase more pear wine from the merchant when he visits," replied Cormac. He opened his mouth to receive the delectable piece of bread.

"It is good," she said between mouthfuls and licking her fingers.

He brushed his finger over her lips. "By the hounds, ye are beautiful, even when ye are eating."

She giggled. "A sticky mess."

Cormac nibbled her chin. "A *sweet* mess. I cannae get enough of ye."

"Even when I'm old and gray?"

Pausing, he cupped her chin. Gazing into those

green eyes, he replied, "Aye. Even after a life with many bairns, I will always want ye."

Eve wrapped her arms around his neck. "Exactly how many babies are we speaking? Two? Three?"

Placing a hand on her abdomen, he replied, "As many as *we* want. I ken how much ye love children, Eve. I want to fill Creag with lots of Murray lads and lasses."

Her eyes softened. "You're serious. And if I want only two?"

Cormac settled her more firmly on his lap. "Then we shall have only two, Eve."

A thoughtful smile curved her mouth. "Well, I happen to know you love children, too." Eve twirled her fingers playfully through the hairs on his chest. "Let's see what happens. I could take forever to get pregnant."

He snorted in amusement. "Nae. Ye already carry my son."

Her mouth dropped open in shock. "Don't tell me you have magical insight into my body?"

Cormac roared with delight. "Call it laird knowledge."

She wiggled trying to free herself. "Arrogant man. Here I was thinking you were like those men, the MacKays—Dragon Knights and you forgot to mention your special power."

He silenced her further protest with his mouth until only soft moans escaped from those luscious lips. Drawing back, he smiled. "When the snows melt in spring, we shall travel to Urquhart Castle to visit the MacKays and their wives."

Chuckling, she said, "It will be great comparing

notes on medieval men."

Cormac rubbed a hand down the back of his neck. "I am doomed already as a husband. Ye will most likely—"

This time Eve silenced him with a whisper of a kiss across his mouth. "I love you, my laird. Now stop talking and make love to me again."

Tossing them both back onto the furs, Cormac happily complied with his wife's orders.

****

Castle Creag—Present Day

As the young couple strolled along the long corridor, they were half-listening to the tour guide explain the many descendants of the Clan Murray at Castle Creag. Their focus was on the portraits and a particular tapestry renowned for its beauty.

Sometimes, they would pause and whisper words to each other. Once, the woman trailed her fingers over the portrait of a girl from the 16th century, and smiled. The man leaned near her and wrapped his arm around her shoulder.

When the rest of the tour and guide left the hall, the couple wandered down to the end. They both glanced at each other with knowing smiles and back up at the huge tapestry hanging on the wall.

"They were a beautiful couple," whispered the woman. "Kind, loving, and generous."

"Yes. One of our finest achievements. How many children did they have?"

"Nine blessed souls." The woman brushed away the tears falling down her cheek. "And to think she wanted to return to her own time."

"Would you have let her come through the veil,

Ailsa?"

"Have I ever told you, Kenan, that I held the door open longer than it should have been?"

He chuckled softly. "No, my love, you have not."

She waved a hand over the tapestry. "I knew Cormac would come for Eve. They only needed a wee bit more time."

Kenan gathered Ailsa into his arms. "All for love," he murmured.

"Always for love."

And in the soft silence of the corridor, the couple vanished.

A Note from the Author

Christmas has always been one of my favorite holidays. I love the preparations—gathering greenery, decorating, sending Christmas cards, and baking. Many years ago, I would start my holiday baking in late September. Yes, you've read correctly. A tradition that began with my mother. All the goodies would be carefully sealed and tucked away in our freezer until the holidays. A truly magical time.

Therefore, it only made sense I would eventually write a story about the holiday season. Cormac Murray was a perfect choice. He was a loyal and true friend of the Dragon Knights, and I loved sending Eve Brannigan to him. She flipped his world upside down, and they both learned lessons about finding and accepting love. I hope you've enjoyed their story.

As a special treat, I've included the recipe that helped Eve win the contest at The Blushing Rose Bakery. It's a treasured recipe in our home, too.

However you celebrate the season, I'm wishing you blessings of love and joy!

Eve Brannigan's Eggnog Scones

2 ½ cups all-purpose flour
1 tablespoon baking powder
½ teaspoon salt
8 tablespoons (1 stick) cold unsalted butter, cut up
1/3 cup sugar
2/3 cup eggnog
2 tablespoons sugar
1 ½ teaspoons fresh or ground nutmeg

Preheat oven to 375 degrees.

Put flour, baking powder, 1 teaspoon nutmeg, and salt into a large bowl. Whisk ingredients.

Add butter and cut in with a pastry blender or rub in with your fingers, until the mixture looks like fine granules. Add sugar and toss to mix.

Add eggnog and stir with a fork until a soft dough forms. Form dough into a ball, put onto a lightly floured board, and give 10 to 12 kneads.

To make triangular scones, cut dough in half. Knead each half lightly into a ball and turn smooth side up. Pat or roll into a 6-inch circle. Cut each circle into 6 or 8 wedges. Place wedges on an ungreased cookie sheet.

Combine sugar with ½ teaspoon nutmeg and sprinkle on wedges. Bake about 12 minutes, or until light brown on top.

A word about the author...

Scottish paranormal romance author, Mary Morgan resides in Northern California, with her own knight in shining armor. However, during her travels to Scotland, England, and Ireland, she left a part of her soul in one of these countries and vows to return.

Mary's passion for books started at an early age along with an overactive imagination. She spent far too much time daydreaming and was told quite often to remove her head from the clouds. It wasn't until the closure of Borders Books where Mary worked that she found her "true calling" writing romance. Now, the worlds she created in her mind are coming to life within her stories.

Visit Mary's website where you'll find links to all of her books, blog, and pictures of her travels.

http://www.marymorganauthor.com

**Other titles by Mary Morgan
available from The Wild Rose Press, Inc.**

Dragon Knight's Sword
Dragon Knight's Medallion
Dragon Knight's Shield
Dragon's Knight's Axe
Dragon Knight's Ring